The Ice Racer

Richard Cozicar

Calgary, Alberta, Canada

www.Richardcozicar.com

ISBN

978-0-9950946-4-2 E-book

978-0-9950946-5-9 Paperback

1. Sci-fi, Y/A, Mystery

This book in its entirety is a work of fiction. People's names, characters, locations and incidents are the product of the author's imagination or are used fictitiously and any similarities or resemblances to real persons, events or settings are wholly coincidental.

Richard Cozicar

Author

Contact Information:

Twitter: @RichardCozicar

www.facebook.com/RichardCozicar

richardcozicar@gmail.com

http://www.richardcozicar.com

Chapter 1

Global warming never happened.

At least not in the way my grandfather explained it to me. That thought floats through my mind while I sit huddled in the lee of a snowdrift, seeking refuge from a monster blizzard raging out of the North. I am totally exhausted after the last few hours of fighting my way through the snowstorm. The irony of my grandfather's words is not lost on me as I struggle to remain awake, my chin incessantly bobbing off my chest.

A moving wall of ash and snow block the world from my view. Defiantly, I stare into the storm, my eyelids drooping from fatigue and the words of my grandfather echoing in my head. Global warming, a warning issued by the Climate Prophets of the early 21st century to the people of the earth, stop the use of fossil fuels or suffer the consequences of escalating temperatures.

The words are like a fairy tale. A solemn history of a bygone world, a written record passed down through the generations of my family. I vividly remember my grandfather telling me how the old world faced a catastrophic battle foretold by scientists using computer models to track the changes of climate patterns.

The specialists grew alarmed by their findings and warned the leaders of the world. The failure to stop the rate of environmental abuse would bring about irreversible damage to the planet. Their theory foretold the melting of the ice caps, which in turn would cause oceans to rise, flooding millions of hectares of habitable coastline. That was the beginning. Other regions of the world, scientists believed, would become nothing more than barren wasteland, unable to sustain any form of life. The warnings went on and on.

I can't help but think how wrong those scientists were.

I lean my head back; the cold winds whine as they howl past. The driven snow is relentless as it swirls around my shelter and continues to isolate me. I lift my gloved hand in front of my face. At less than a foot from my eyes, my hand disappears in the blanket of ash-gray powder. I'm still too exhausted to move. My head sags and I find myself watching the large white flakes as they settle over my body; my thoughts return to those words of long ago.

The world leaders ignored the science, and that led to the rise of the Climate Prophets. The environmentalists lectured about the continued use of carbon-based fuels. Over time the world became divided between those who believed they were saving the planet and those who chose to ignore the warnings. The prophets used fear to recruit followers and with numbers came power.

When the movement controlled armies, they declared war against the denying governments. A fierce battle began that would push humanity to the brink of extinction.

The prophets proclaimed that renewable energy would be the only accepted source of fuel. The clean energy was comprised of massive steel turbines erected to catch the blowing winds. These metal towers began covering the earth; solar farms were used to catch the sun's rays, and geothermal heat from deep within the earth would now help power civilization.

I remember something my grandfather said to me years ago. His stories always began with a smile as he fondly reminisced about the days of his youth. "Mike," he would say. "I remember my grandpa telling me that there was a time, not long before he was born, when children just like you could venture outdoors and play all day under bright blue skies with their friends, the lot of them wearing only the flimsiest of clothes.

He told me that back in those days, children didn't need thermal suits. They played in sunshine and rain on the grass-covered ground and in forests of green trees. In fact, if I recall correctly, sometimes my grandpa even talked about a type of short pants, pants that came above the knees. Kids would run about under the open skies without socks or shoes on their feet. And every time my grandfather told this story he would stop, and I could see in his eyes the dreams of a world so long ago, a world I think he tried to conjure in his mind much different than the world that existed today.

My grandfather was old, and I never questioned him because I treasured our time together. I often wondered if his aging mind invented these stories, or if his great grandpa had shared these tales with him. Sometimes I would lay by his side and close my eyes dreaming right along with him of the wonderful world that existed, if only in his mind.

I knew he was on in years and his memories probably confused, but still, the way he described his dream of clear skies and soft grass where kids could roam out doors free of protective clothing sounded a lot like heaven. When I asked my dad about grandfather's stories, my dad would laugh and remind me not to take the old guy too seriously. My father was practical. He would often warn me not to waste my life daydreaming about a long forgotten world with sunshine and blue skies, when in reality the topside of our planet was barren, deadly tundra.

The surface of the planet is snow covered, cold and void of life. The hottest time of the year is summer, when the temperature may climb as warm as minus fifty, much too cold for a person to even consider walking the caves of our city without the warmth of a thin heat suit.

The thought of minus fifty temperatures jolts me back to my current dilemma. The storm has increased in strength. The blowing snow has collected over my outstretched legs while I rest. It seems like the winds are determined to erase any evidence of my existence from the surface. I keep my head down; the frozen pellets scrape across my visor. The wind moans and howls past my helmet and its icy fingers tug at the fabric of my thermal suit.

The ferocity of this storm worries me. For the last several months, I have noticed that the intensity of these blizzards has been building.

Something ominous is driving the increase in activity, almost like the winds are trying to blow everything off the face of the planet. Whatever the outcome, it can't be good. Not when the surface is as deadly as this.

I'm tired. My energy sapped. I tell myself a couple more minutes then I'd better move. The muscles in my legs still burn from slogging through the high drifts and fresh accumulation of grey snow. Shortly after I recovered from the fall off my ship and picked myself off the ground, I have been chasing after the ice sled. At first, I was able to follow in the depressions left by the wide metal skis of the heavy ship, but the wind and snow conspired against me. Not long into my walk, the tracks began to fill in. The blizzard was erasing the trail.

Every step was a struggle. How many times I sank body deep into yards of the fresh powder, I can't recall. Each time I would have to swim back to the top, feel around for solid footing and then start walking again. More than once I fought back to the top utterly exhausted and contemplated giving up and letting the storm claim me. Each time, a voice inside screamed for me to stand up and continue my journey.

The tracks had disappeared hours ago. I kept walking. I tried to mark the ice sled's direction in my mind and stubbornly forged on, but in my heart, I knew I was fighting a losing battle.

Dwelling on my earlier ordeals distract me while I rest, stranded in the middle of this frozen sea with only drifts and ice hills to keep me company. The drifts built by the ceaseless winds, the hills of ice formed by decades of repeated cycles of snow and sub-zero temperatures. I swipe my glove across the front of my visor removing the accumulating powder, but the wall of flakes still obscures my view. Not that there would be much to look at other than an endless sea of shifting snow.

The frozen pellets hammer at my helmet and scrape across my visor while the cold wind shrieks and pulls at my clothing. I ignore the disturbance. Monitoring the readout displayed on the inside of my mask, I check on the battery life powering my thermal suit. The batteries are wired into the fabric and recharge as I walk. My movements over the last few hours as I pushed through the drifting snow did little to restore them. But if I alternate between turning the suit on and off, I may be able to prolong the inevitable. By rationing the remaining power, I can extend the batteries long enough to survive until I find a way out of this vast collection of snow dunes. If not, then I will succumb to the cold.

The protection of my suit leaves me a small chance of survival.

I say a slight possibility because I am in hostile territory. Funny, I think. Anywhere outside the massive caves of the New Capital is considered unfriendly territory. Hostile in the fact that anyone stranded alone on the surface will undoubtedly perish, if not from some unseen enemy, then from the unbridled cruelty of this frozen sphere we call earth.

I think back to earlier in the day, when I was piloting the ice sled. The crew and I were on a return trip to the New Capital with a desperately needed cargo of fuel and food supplies. We had scavenged the cargo from a site several days travel from our home. A massive storm blew out of nowhere. A blizzard we tried to outrun even though we knew the odds of travelling ahead of the storms edge were small.

Just as we figured it would, the storm bore down on us, and as the pilot, I tried to force the sled through. When you are an Ice Racer, your job is to deliver. Being delayed by these storms meant undue hardships for both the crew and ship and with limited power supplies, any length of a delay could leave the whole lot of us stranded. Besides, the Capital was in dire need of the cargo. I had no choice but to risk running the storm.

I left my co-pilot manning the rudder while I ventured outside to fix one of the sails damaged by the hurricane-force winds. Stepping out of the cabin onto the sled's deck, I was stunned by the ferocity of the gale. The wind and snow tore at my footing. I was well aware of the risks, but it was my ship and my crew. They, along with the people back at our settlement, depended on me.

I had barely finished the repairs when the sled careered off the edge of an ice hill camouflaged by the storm. The ship tilted sideways tossing me overboard. With the savagery of the blizzard, I knew that by the time my crew realized I was gone, any form of rescue had already passed. For my team to turn around and search for me would put the ship and their lives in jeopardy. The loss of one person was better than having the whole ship and crew disappear on this run.

I realized and accepted that fact; the reality had been burned into all our minds when we trained for these missions on the surface. I was not the first person to be lost on one of these voyages, and I certainly won't be the last.

I don't know the amount of time that had elapsed since the sled disappeared; but it must have been hours that I walked braced against the savagery of the storm. Eventually the winds calmed from hurricane force to a less vicious howl.

My suit has a backup air supply, but like the thermal heat, I have to use it sparingly, so the batteries don't run dead.

I instinctively turned on my emergency air supply and dug myself out of the loose powder in time to watch the back of the sled vanish into the blizzard. I attempted to pursue the ship, but after a few futile steps, where I sank to my waist, I realized that option no longer existed. I dropped to my knees to formulate a plan. At first, I thought about simply digging in and waiting out the storm. The reasoning was sound, but the winds were blowing large amounts of fresh snow, it would be only a matter of time before the sled's trail would be erased. Even for the few minutes I remained motionless and contemplated my next move, a fresh layer of powder fell over me. At least the snow helped insulate against the frigid temperatures.

I found my footing and began walking until I stumbled upon this windbreak, too weary to march on.

Every man and woman from the New Capital who ventures onto the ice sleds has a survival kit attached to our suits. The packs contain food rations, a thermal shovel, and a few small heat pods. We trained for unexpected emergencies, but adapting the theories in real life-and- death situations are worlds apart. Stranded on the top of this unforgiving cap of ice and wind, the only things I can rely on are common sense and my refusal to surrender.

I decrease the suit's air supply while I rest. I toggle the heat function off and on in intervals to prolong the life of the batteries. I patiently wait, the snow piling higher. I sense the winds decreasing, so I think of digging out of the drift. Shelter from the conditions will be a priority, somewhere safe to ride out the night. I do have to admit that in all my years of piloting a sled, I have never noticed anything that resembled a haven, only endless windblown plains of deadly shifting landscapes. I postpone moving, telling myself I'll wait a few more minutes. The exhaustion of my trek still weighs heavy on me.

*****

I must have fallen asleep. My eyes flash open, my body shivering uncontrollably. The biting cold has seeped past the outer layer of my thermal suit. I push myself away from the drift, the fresh snow that has cloaked me falls away. I stand on weary legs. It's time I move and find a place to spend the night. If I march in the direction I believe will lead back toward home I can search for shelter along the way. My hope is to locate a sizeable ice hill where I can burrow deep inside and escape the elements. After that, all I can do is pray that I have enough resources to keep me alive for the next couple of days.

Fortunately, it is still day, although daylight is a bit of a misnomer. The distinction between day and night only means that the dark is a lighter shade of black. All my life, this is the only 'daylight' I have known. As I grew up, my grandfather regaled me with stories of an earlier time where the skies were clear and blue and the only time the sun didn't shine was when rain clouds blocked its rays. Not so in today's world.

"But that all changed during the middle of the 21st century," he would sadly end his tale. As the Climate Prophet's armies marched across the globe in their drive to end the use of fossil fuels, they left behind fields of metal towers that reached hundreds of feet into the skies and channelled the blowing winds to produce energy for the power-starved planet.

Before the end of the great Climate War, the combined shaking of all these turbines caused rifts in the land to open and then the vibrations travelled deep into the earth's core, disrupting the planet's stability. A series of eruptions followed as long-dormant volcanoes exploded to life, spewing lava and plumes of ash. The toxic ash poured upward, flooding the atmosphere and choking out the sun. The grey clouds thickened and over several decades blocked the sun's rays from reaching the earth. Since that time, the distinction between night and day varied little. It has been this way for a very long time.

I shake the memories from my head and step into the teeth of the raging storm, leaving the temporary shelter of the snowdrift. The odds against my surviving in this unforgiving hell are small, but as long as I can still function, I refuse to give up hope. No one ever lost on this frozen tundra has ever been seen again. I hope to change that. I don't believe in miracles, but now, I think, would be a good time for one.

Chapter 2

The Long Cold Walk

A couple more hours have now passed since I left the snowdrift and resumed my trek. Camouflaged areas of snow are so loose that I sink to my chest. Every move is arduous, and my steps are now more a shuffle than a walk. One foot in front of the other, I plough through banks of snow. I keep the wind at my side, the same direction I had steered the ice sled. At times, I use my arms to pull my body over pools too deep to walk. The one saving grace is that the atmosphere is dry and the snow doesn't pack easily.

I force my legs to move, my breathing laboured as I push on. I wade through the white expanse, partially blinded. Along with the driving snow, the warmth of my exhaled breath obscures my sight. It fogs my visor, the warm air I release condensing when it meets the cold winds buffeting against my helmet.

The unrelenting wind is the thing I find the most disturbing. It tugs at the fabric of my suit and shifts the snow, continuously reshaping the area around me. The wind whines as it blows over the open plains and past my head. I can't escape the haunting moan in my ears. At times, the wind tricks my mind by giving the impression of stealing my breath, even though I'm protected inside my helmet. The wind never lets up.

I march on.

When I left the snowdrift, I chose a direction I hoped would lead me closer to the New Capital. In all honesty, I have no idea if I am heading on the right path, only my instincts to guide me. All around are endless miles of ash-blended snow broken by the random bulge of snowdrifts. There is nothing tangible to help me navigate. Volcanic ash permanently blurs the sky; there is no way to know what direction I am walking, no sun to follow, and no landmarks to guide me. For all I know, I could be moving in a large circle.

With each step, I move onward, my eyes fixed straight ahead on an imaginary horizon. Being the pilot of an ice sled, I have developed a sixth sense in regards to directions. I am somewhat confident that I am on the right course, but only time will tell.

I came to grip with reality the moment the storm shook me off the deck of the ice sled. I am lost and will more than likely perish in this desolate, merciless landscape, and the continually blowing snow will eventually bury me. If I were smart, I would sit down and conserve my energy as I wait for the last breath to leave my body, but I guess I'm not that smart.

To become the pilot of an ice sled, a person has to have an unyielding sense of survival and an undaunted willingness to persevere. I was at the top of the class when those attributes were needed. Again, maybe I am not all that smart.

I trudge thru the waist-deep drifts and reflect on how I ended up stranded on the surface, separated from my ship and crew. I try to keep my mind busy. The encompassing snow and screaming winds will otherwise drive me mad.

Few people living in the New Capital are suited or volunteer for being a crewmember on an ice sled. It is the one job that is a near-perfect guarantee to get you killed. Very few members of society have ever ventured out and walked on or even seen the earth's surface. People are afraid to leave the safety of our ice-domed city for one reason. The environment above our ice dwellings is a harsh, bitter place to survive.

As a teenager, I volunteered and trained for work on the sleds. My father had piloted one of our sleds and while out on a run, failed to return. He vanished along with his crew days before I turned sixteen. Over the last five years, I have strived to become the best pilot in our group. I found my fear of the surface much less than the fear of remaining hidden underground and barely subsisting, going through the motions and waiting to die. For that reason, I am willing to take risks that others find too dangerous.

I figured being top side and facing the elements couldn't be any worse than cowering in caves buried deep beneath the frozen layers of snow. I felt trapped in the confines of the frozen city. I missed my father and wanted an opportunity to find him. I needed hope and an avenue of escape.

Life in the New Capital is hard. Every day is a struggle. We fight to keep from freezing, grapple with the shortage of food and struggle just to make it to another day. The people of the New Capital do the best they can, but we are a civilization trying to rebuild. The great climate wars of the 21st century decimated life on earth and now we are pitted against an environment that turned hostile. We work arduously to prolong life.

The living conditions are the reason we have sled teams willing to risk their necks. Every time one leaves our small community and ventures onto the frozen plains, their odds decrease. Ours is a continuous search for fuel to aid our survival. We have precious little and what we do have is rigidly guarded and rationed among the several thousand occupants that call the New Capital home.

The transportation of fuel and supplies is where I come in.

Several generations ago, explorers from the Capital stumbled across a buried cache of oil and gas reserves. Since that discovery, the job of the ice racers has been to brave the elements and replenish the dwindling fuel supply at the New Capital. Only a few of these metal ice sleds remain, and with their small size and our inadequate energy sources, we can transport a limited amount of fuel at a time. It's a vicious circle.

The trips can average weeks, so by the time we find our way back with the cargo, we have to turn around and head out again. We would build bigger sleds, but materials are in short supply. If we are lucky, the blowing wind will expose one of the metal wind towers that our ancestors erected hundreds of years ago. These huge metal windmills once covered the earth's surface but now lay buried deep beneath tons of snow and ice.

On occasion, one of the sled crews may accidentally stumbled across the odd metal behemoth exposed by the shifting winds. The discovering sled team takes great effort to mark the location for a crew of inventor's to follow and cannibalize the rig of its precious metals and wires. However, most times the snow and the wind are quicker to reclaim what they uncover than our people are at returning to the site. Such is life. But it is our life, and we keep going.

The pain in my legs stops my reminiscing and switches my focus back to my predicament. My muscles are burning from the struggle through the snow. The permeating cold sends shivers throughout my body. The exertion from my struggle has helped stave off the risk of hypothermia and prolonged the life of the batteries. But once I stop, I will need power to heat the suit.

Dark is turning darker, and I prefer not to sit down and wait out the night while the storm envelops me. In the failing light, a break in the blizzard reveals a rise in the ground ahead. A mirage no doubt, but with luck it may be a hill of solid ice I've been searching for. A place I can burrow into and escape the storm's wrath for the night.

Willing my legs to move one shuffling step at a time, I head for the protrusion hoping my eyes are not playing tricks on me. I focus on the bulge in the grey snow, afraid that if I blink, the hill will vanish. The muscles in my legs quiver from exertion, my breath in rasps. I am so worn from the hours of battling the blizzard the cold is temporarily forgotten.

One step follows another. My movements are mechanical. The next step is onto a freshly covered crevasse. The ground under my foot disappears and I sink into the yawning pit of dirty snow. I tumble and flail about, swimming back to the top. I climb in a flash of panic, my head swivels frantically to relocate the ice hill. The dark is all- consuming now, pushing at the limits of my sight. I peer from behind the light enhancement of my visor through the whipping snow and inky darkness. With a surge of pure determination, I fight my way out of the bowl scrambling until my feet contact solid ground. I push forward.

My efforts are rewarded and I approach the mound. One foot slips on the side of the hill sending me crashing down. I struggle to my knees. Too tired to even think I kneel in the snow at the base of the hill to catch my breath and give my over burdened muscles a reprieve. Within minutes, the numbing cold seeps back into my thermal suit reminding me to hurry and find shelter from the coming night.

I grip the handle of my thermal shovel and remove it from my pack then start sweeping aside the looser snow before plunging the heated blade into the ice. I start carving an opening. Fighting back fatigue I tunnel into the ice that forms the hill. I dig and shovel cutting a path upwards. Several feet into the hill I change directions and begin tunnelling downward. The purpose of the change in direction is to keep the wind from entering. I pause to rest. The strain on my body helps ward off some of the bone-chilling temperatures. With renewed effort I push the shovel into the hill, the heated blade melting through the ice. I need to burrow deep enough into the hill that I leave the wind and cold behind.

Time passes, I stop tunnelling. I must be at least ten feet down. The wind no longer tugs at my suit. I use the shovel to melt and remove excess ice. The hole grows bigger. I now have room to turn comfortably, but not so big that my heating pod can't warm the space. I lean the shovel aside, then rifle through my pack.

Activating a heat source, I sit with my back against an ice wall, my muscles protesting from abuse.

It a good thing I'm used to talking to myself, otherwise I would go crazy. Outside the tunnel entrance, the wind howls. Letting my mind dwell on my situation is too dangerous. I try to occupy my mind by rummaging through my supplies. Pulling out a food packet, I fasten it to the feeding tube in my helmet.

Food in our community is a simple matter. It starts with a moss that grows on the edges of the lava flows near our city. The purple lichen is dried and added to our meagre supply of vegetables grown in the city's greenhouses. The combination ground and stored for use. I puncture the package and draw the substance into my helmet through a feeding apparatus. When the powder comes in contact with the saliva in my mouth, it expands into chewable semi-solid form. I don't know if it tastes good or not, because it's the only food I have ever eaten. I'm exhausted and starved. At this very moment, the food is the best I've ever eaten.

I settle back against the wall of the cave and reach a hand into a front pocket of my suit. My searching fingers find my reading page. The battery symbol flashes on the page when I power it up. I waver between charging the paper with my suit and further depleting the battery supply, or facing a night alone with the worry of being stranded.

After a brief debate, I decide to charge the reading page. I'm lucky to have it along to keep me company. Reading pages are scarce in our city. My grandfather set it into my hands shortly before he died. He advised me to keep the paper secret. "Even from your father," he warned. The elders would confiscate the reading page if they discovered it in my possession. And yet, stranded as I am, I'm lucky to have a means of distraction.

This reading page had been passed down from a long-deceased ancestor to my great grandfather and then to his son, my grandfather and now I guard it. I keep the page hidden in my suit at all times. I jealously hide its existence and have never mentioned it to my father for fear of losing it. From the moment I began reading the historical memoirs in the diary, I came to realize that my grandfather's tales were not simply the ramblings of an old, feeble mind. The journal documented the tragic history of humanity's march toward extinction.

A distant relative, Jeff Ryan, had begun recording the journal back in the middle of the 21st century. The man was a captain during the last war fought on earth, a battle that pitted the peoples' army against the steadily growing armies of the Climate Prophets.

The page lights up. I start reading a random entry.

Chapter 3

The Diary

July 3, 2044

We continued training with troops from the European Union. Our allies arrived a week ago, and we are anticipating rigorous drills for the next three weeks preparing for war against the forces of the Climate Prophets.

The war was totally unexpected. At first, the governments of the world had not taken the radical threats seriously, writing the group off as annoying fanatics. The Climate army's now number in the millions and is proving to be a dangerous adversary with their expanding reach and co-ordinated attacks.

The prophets have been hugely successful in recruiting large numbers of volunteers with promises of a green planet, the continued opposition to fossil fuels and a dogged campaign of bombing strategic world oil reserves. The terrorist actions by these organized groups are now having a devastating effect on the continued harvesting and transportation of necessary supplies. At the rate that the attacks are occurring most countries are now struggling to maintain day-to-day operations.

I was informed yesterday of my new promotion. I will now be the youngest captain in the Canadian Army at 23 years of age. I was born in the U.S., but shortly after my mother moved to Canada. My father, Charles M. Ryan died months before I was born. Mom told me he died a hero while saving the president of the United States.

Captain Jeff Ryan. Cool. The promotion has a nice ring to it. But my celebration is short-lived. Our world forces are collapsing under the determined advances of the Climate Prophets and their growing anti-oil army.

I received news this morning that my training here in Wainwright will be cut short. I am to report as a Canadian liaison to the American Army at Yakima Training Center in Washington State. There, I will join fellow officers from across the continent to devise plans for the retaking of American fuel reserves that the enemy has captured.

I hate to leave at this time. Since the rains of June have stopped, we've experienced nothing but blue skies and plenty of sunshine; the temperatures are climbing into the high twenties. The moisture has turned everything green, and the air is clean and fresh.

I close my eyes and try to imagine the beautiful world described in the pages. I wonder what fresh air after a shower of rain would smell like or grass under my feet and the rays of the sun on my face?

My daydream is interrupted by reality as the bitter cold touches the tips of my fingers and chills my toes. I scan the readouts on my visor. While I was tunnelling into the hill, I switched off the batteries to conserve power, but forgot to turn them back on.

Wearily, I climb to my feet and move around inside of my small ice cave, swinging my arms and stomping my feet to drive out the encroaching chill. I'm restless. Even though I accepted the terms with my situation while I trekked through the snow, the desolation is hard to accept. I've never been alone before and have certainly never been outside of the city and above ground by myself. No one has. I'm afraid I don't quite know how to deal with this.

Heat radiates from the elements sewn into my suit and starts to warm my limbs. I sit back down using the wall of my small cave as a backrest. I need to keep my mind busy, so the feelings of doubt and despair don't paralyze me.

Picking up the reading paper, I swipe my gloved hand across the screen and stop at a page in the diary hoping the words will keep my mind busy.

June 10, 2045

The Climate Prophet's armies are growing exponentially. The world governments are losing the battle. Climate armies are burning and destroying all our sources of fuel at an alarming rate. Their actions are forcing us to retreat on many fronts. The lack of fuel is slowing and in some cases stopping our progress to protect strategic oil deposits around the world.

Today the European president ordered a significant number of troops to pull back and defend the remaining caches of oil they still control. The Climate armies have since invaded the Saudi Conglomerate States, decimating the Saudi armies and destroying vast tracts of the Middle Eastern oil fields.

The forces of our enemy have embraced the strategy of starving the rest of us of all fossil fuels. Not only is this affecting the army's united against them, but also it's created a shortage for the oil thirsty population invoking worldwide rationing. For the time being, the only manufacturing left untouched by the ration is the munitions factories.

People by the thousands and soon millions will be without work and soon, they will be without the necessary supplies to operate their vehicles and heat their homes

If the war continues to drag on, everyone but the people fortunate enough to be enlisted in the military will be left to fend for themselves. The army can't fight off the Climate forces and at the same time maintain the peace in the countries being ravaged by the energy shortage. I am afraid that anarchy will soon overtake us.

October 5, 2045

Everywhere our unit travels we come upon caravans of displaced families, their few possessions in tow. Parents hold tight to their children as they watch us drive past, lines of worry etched on their faces. In their eyes, you can see the pride that refuses to let them beg for assistance. Jobs are becoming scarce, and the military has stopped recruiting. We are no longer able to accommodate the growing stream of applicants who were signing up as a means of supporting their families.

Travelling through the major cities is disheartening. There is no more room for the influx of travellers who arrive daily. Factories and high-rises are becoming deserted. Since the power grids were shut down, the structures lay barren, the buildings stripped of any useful materials and the streets filled with homeless families. Adding to the dilemma, the late-fall weather is turning cold. Winter is not far off and very few families have the essentials necessary to survive the coming cold months.

October 7, 2045

Plumes of smoke rise all around us. The air is thick and a haze from the many fires stings my eyes. The blanketing smog burns my lungs with every breath I take. Most of us have taken to wearing bandanas wrapped over our faces, the cloth tied tight around our nose and mouths. Now that the snow and cold have drifted down from the North, people have resorted to burning whatever materials they can scrounge for warmth.

Everywhere I turn, I see reminders of where wooden structures once lay, the buildings stripped of all flammable materials right down to the concrete foundations. Piles of refuse mark the destroyed homes like grave markers. And now even the residents we were sent to protect watch us suspiciously as we pass, their loyalty wavering against us in their desperate fight to exist.

Law and order is this country is crumbling and things most people believed sacred are slipping by the wayside. The assault on libraries is one of these. Protection of reading materials has fallen under the army's jurisdiction. Volunteer groups in each community help the army guard the historical books, but with the need for heating fuels increasing, the defense of these bastions of written wisdom will inevitably fall.

October 15,2045

We were passing through a small city in Central Alberta. Dark clouds of smoke drift into the sky from the centre of town. We hurried to the scene. People rushed about the street. The townsfolk formed a bucket brigade and were passing pails of water to fight a blaze that had engulfed a pair of houses. I jumped out of my transport and waved men from my unit to help.

Screams came from one of the houses. I rushed past the line of buckets and peered into the roaring inferno. Another scream. This one was a cry from a small child. I moved closer to the house. An older gentleman grabbed my arm to hold me back. He sadly shook his head and pulled me away. Within seconds the roof collapsed, shooting sparks outward, some falling on a neighbouring house. As I stood there helplessly watching, the next house began smouldering.

"Where in the hell is the fire department," I asked the man. He glanced at me and then turned back toward the fire.

"There is no fire department left in this town," he grimly replied.

Every day on our journey, reports filtered back to my regiment with horrific stories of men, women, and children succumbing to carbon monoxide poisoning, numerous others dying in fires that blaze out of control, as families desperately try to heat their homes and escape the cold of the approaching winter. I'm not aware of too many fire departments that remain in most of these towns and cities. A lot have been destroyed or had their equipment and fuel supplies stolen. Still, it would be unlikely of many to venture out to fight house fires, the fuel they are allotted needs to lay in wait for more severe responses. What that is... I'm not certain.

October 30, 2045

We were met with bad news when we awoke this morning. A great portion of Europe has fallen to the climate armies. The defeat came only weeks after the sacking of the Saudi Conglomerate States and the destruction of the Middle Eastern oil reserves. The growing armies of the Climate Prophets have marched north. The numbers of their ranks have swelled by millions, swayed with promises of shelter and food for the upcoming winter. Energy is power these days. If you have it, you make the rules for society.

Analysts predict that the siege of the United Kingdom is only weeks, at the most a month away, and the majority of soldiers across the North American continent are being deployed to the eastern seaboards. There, the extra bodies will be required to reinforce our defenses. Preparations for when the climate armies head west with their impending surge from across the ocean. We have not received any oil shipments from abroad for months now, and our fuel supplies have dwindled. I will be part of a unit left behind to protect the oil fields in Alberta and the Dakotas.

So far the unity of the western provinces and states has been able to limit the amount of damage. But the environmental movement is growing in strength. Their plan is to divide us. It will take a monumental effort to keep the remaining resources from falling into the hands of the enemy.

We can't expect help from the South Americans, either. No country is immune from the Prophet's armies. The South American governments have banded together and are currently locked in a fierce battle of their own. The last report from the southern hemisphere is that the war has pushed far inland, and large tracts of the country's resources have been destroyed by the roaming Climate Prophet's armies.

I turn the reading paper off as my eyelids flicker closed. I power down my suit. The long walk today has taken its toll on me. I fight to remain awake, worried that if I do fall asleep, it may well be for the last time. But the exhaustion from my trek is overwhelming. I compromise and lean my head back, reassuring myself I'll only close my eyes for a minute. Images flash in my head. I focus on pleasant thoughts filled with sunny skies and green grass, trees blowing in the breeze and the laughter of children. Why, I wonder, would our predecessors who lived in a warm and luxurious haven resembling paradise, want to destroy everything they had built? This thought is even more unsettling to me than being alone and stranded on the surface of this dead planet.

I drift off into a chilled, restless sleep. My dreams waver between a warm, hospitable planet and the white, frozen world of today. Images roll into nightmares. My sleep is uneasy. In one scene, I am walking barefoot over hills of swaying grass with the sun high above me. The next minute a north wind brings dark clouds and snow. The grassy fields morph into the ice and cold of today's world. My bare skin grows chilled as I walk and then suddenly the ground beneath my feet shakes. A large crack appears, and I fall into the abyss.

Awakened by the reality of my dreams, my eyes dart open. It's dark. Through my glove, I feel water on the floor beside me. The lack of light in the cave adds to the vividness of the nightmare, leaving me shaken. I turn my head slowly staring into the dark space that surrounds me. A dull glow of orange to the side of my feet catches my eye. The light radiates from the blade of my thermal shovel. I curse for having forgotten to turn it off. I am still drowsy. Then the floor shifts again. Maybe I am still sleeping. The groaning of fractured ice echoes in the cave and the floor gives way. It wasn't a dream. Suddenly, I AM falling.

Chapter 4

River Of Red

My mouth opens wide in shock, and my voice rings in my ears. The crack in the floor widens, sending me tumbling into the darkness, my arms swinging at the air. I land hard, the breath driven from my body. I bounce awkwardly, and then lay still as I try to refill my lungs. I have come to rest on a slick, solid surface well below the ice hill. I continue sucking in mouthfuls of air to calm my racing heart. Lying on my back, I carefully stretch out my hands and slide them around, feeling the area around me before I risk moving. Echoes of my fall tell me I'm in a cave, one that is much larger than the hole I had dug. In case I am lying on a cliff or shelf or who knows what, I resist the urge to stand quickly. I don't want to fall again.

I can see the glowing blade of my shovel through the opening. I scramble as the shovel slices through the dark, hurtling after me. The heated rim of the blade appears larger as it drops. I straighten my arm, my fingers scrambling to find traction against the slick surface. With a grunt, I push hard and roll out of the path of the blade. The shovel smashes into the ice inches from where I lay. Sitting up, I stretch my arm to reach for the shovel, while plunging my other hand into my suit, my fingers searching for a light.

I swing the light this way and that, it's beam stabbing through the darkness to illuminate sections of the cavern. I seem to have fallen into an expansive ice cave, one probably caused by trapped air when the ice hill originally formed.

The floor is slick. My hands and my feet slide out from under me as I try to stand. Losing my footing, I topple forward and crash face first to the floor. My visor smacks the ice, the shovel flies from my fingertips. I lay sprawled on my stomach, the front of my helmet tight to the frozen surface. Dazed, I stare straight down. I grow increasingly nervous when I realize I am looking through a transparent floor. Far below me, a faint red ribbon winds across the dark.

I remain motionless, letting my brain piece together the sight below. A loud snap reverberates off the cave walls and the floor trembles, the ribbon below temporarily forgotten. The ice I'm laying on shifts a fraction and then holds. My breath catches in my throat, my heart rate quickens. Very gently, I start to climb to my feet.

The ice groans a warning seconds before the floor gives way. For the second time in minutes, I find myself tumbling through the blackness. The faint glow that was far below me is growing brighter as I tumble through space.

At this point, I'm not even sure if I am awake or dreaming. The darkness blots out everything but the glow from the ribbon, which grows redder as I somersault downward. My throat is raw from screaming, and I become aware of an updraft pressing against the fabric of my suit.

The scene is surreal. My brain tells me I am falling, but within the encompassing darkness, I feel as I'm floating. The only perception of movement is the red ribbon looming closer.

Seconds, minutes, I'm not certain how long I spiral downward. I struggle to inflate my suit to its full capacity, hoping that this will help cushion my fall.

I think I'm screaming. The fear and adrenaline overload my senses, sending me into the safety of unconsciousness. My eyes flutter open briefly, shaken awake when I hit the ground with a bone-jarring impact. The air built up in my suit cushions a portion of the crash, and before I pass out again, I am aware of my body bouncing before it settles.

Consciousness creeps into the void of blackness. My fluttering eyelids signal my return to the present, and my senses respond. Dazed and confused, I lay motionless, letting my brain navigate the fog of uncertainty. The steady beat of my heart comforts me until snippets of the fall from above flash in my head and my pulse increases.

I move uncomfortably, my left arm pinned awkwardly beneath me, and a layer of sweat coats my body. How is this possible? My muddled thoughts fish for an answer. The New Capital, the cabin on the ice sled…hell, the whole planet is nothing more than a frozen ball of ice. The only reason a person would sweat…memories of the red ribbon resurface. I sit up quickly to check my surroundings, the movements too fast for my sluggish condition because my head swims and a wave of nausea roils deep in my stomach.

My unconsciousness dissipates and I feel a bolt of pain shooting up the arm I landed on. The intense pain blocks out my previous thoughts and pushes me closer to another blackout. Sweat drips from my forehead and my teeth are tightly clenched as I grimace against the discomfort and gently wiggle my fingers. Jolts of electricity race like fire in my nerves, sending alarms screaming into my brain. Fractured but not broken, I diagnose, and then let my arm hang still.

My mind clears, but my vision remains blurred. I bring my right hand up to the front of my visor. All I can see is a distorted image. I shake my head side to side to drive the lingering fog from my brain and concentrate. The inside of my faceplate swims into focus. My eyesight seems fine, so something must be wrong with the outside of my visor. Swiping my hand across the front of the helmet only makes my visibility worse. My gloved hand is adding to the problem; so I use my sleeve and scrub the front of my visor clean and gaze down at my hand.

Mud. Soupy, black soil covers the palm of my glove and the legs of my thermal suit. Again, I wonder how this can be possible? Struggling against the suction of the soft earth, I straighten up and study the ground. The only place I know of that has enough heat to cause sweat and warm the soil is...I rise to my knees and scan the area. Twisting around, I look behind and discover the source of heat needed to melt the frozen earth. The ribbon I had seen from the cave floor above is a river of liquid rock.

A shimmering stream of lava meanders not more than a hundred feet from where I landed, flowing from between rising banks of rock. From this distance I have no way of knowing if the banks are rock or cooled lava. I am too far away to see clearly in the poor light thrown off by the river's red glow. The heat from the melted lava would certainly explain the film of moisture coating my skin.

Swinging my leg under me, I brace my foot and rise from the soft muck. My boot slides and I instinctively reach with my fractured arm to steady my body. White bursts of light flash before my eyes as I fall face down in the muck, my teeth clenched while a wave of pain floods my brain. Minutes pass before I build the courage to climb to my feet a second time. My good arm braced for support, I push away from the soft ground.

From my knees, I use my hand for balance, and I half walk and half crawl up an embankment away from the stream of lava. The footing is slick, and the ground sucks at my boots. The heat from the ribbon of red behind me is intense. The greater the distance, the more the air begins to cool. Soon the soft soil gives way to jagged patches of cooled lava. When my boots grip onto the solid ground, I stop and look back. I've climbed up a rise, leaving the river far enough behind that the cold cavern air offers respite from the heat. The faint light from the flowing lava barely reaches the darkness this far up as I look for a place to sit and evaluate my condition.

I know that my arm is in rough shape, and the pain from it might be blocking out other receptors in my body. I know my injuries will reveal themselves once the shock from the fall wears off. I take the pain in my arm as a good sign that my other injuries aren't as severe.

I will need a strap from my pack to fasten my injured arm tight to the front of my suit. Then it dawns on me. I twist my right hand behind my back and feel for my emergency kit. I let out a sigh. My shovel and flashlight slipped from my grasp when I fell, but my pack seems intact.

I grit my teeth and gingerly slide the kit from around my shoulders, taking precautions with my injury. With the pack in front of me, I breathe deep to quell the pain shooting from my throbbing arm. I place the backpack between my knees and undo the flap, searching for my medical supplies. Slipping the pain reliever from the pack, I lift it to the intake apparatus built into my helmet. The tube is shattered, broken by my fall.

The heating modules and breathing filter in my helmet escaped damaged, and the light modifier in my helmet is still functioning. But the system that allows me to eat and drink didn't fare as well. Now, the only way to take the medication may well be for me remove my visor. On the surface, this would result in death from the sub-zero temperatures, but probably not so in the heat of this buried cavern. My worry is the toxicity of the air in this space. I have no way to know if the vapours rising off the running lava are poisonous.

I stare down the hill toward the visible thin red line of the river and review my options, the awful pain clouding my thoughts too much to ignore. I have no choice but to open my helmet so I can swallow the medicine. If I am quick, I should be able to quickly reseal it before I breathe in the cavern air.

Rehearsing the moves in my head, I plan out the steps needed to accomplish this feat. Laying a foil pouch of nutrition on my knee for easy access, I hesitate, and then touch the clasps on the front of my helmet. My fingers shake as I loosen the seal. Dragging a chest full of filtered air deep into my lungs, I hold my breath and quickly flip open the faceplate.

My hand drops to my knee and I snatch the waiting packet, lifting it to my mouth. Jamming the corner of the envelope in my teeth, I bite and tear to rip it open. It takes longer than I planned. My chest starts bucking as my lungs fight for air. I tug at the packet and succeed to rip it open. A small portion of the white powder leaks from the envelope, but the rest I manage to pour into my mouth.

Dropping the foil, I slam the plate of my visor shut, my movements awkward, hampered by the use of only one hand. I can't hold my breath any longer. As is human nature, I gasp and then involuntarily gulp a mouthful of cavern air, filling my lungs before I can safely replace my visor. With trembling fingers, I seal my helmet and wait to see if the air is poisonous.

Seconds pass, my breathing calms.

Tension subsides as time marches. In the back of my mind, I imagine myself falling to the ground violently ill. I am not sure what the effects of breathing poison air would do to my body or if the symptoms would be instant or slowly poison me over time. Back at the New Capital, the same volcano that supplies heat for the city also contaminates our air. Therefore, I have never taken a breath without the safety of my helmet.

The pain in my arm is temporarily forgotten while I puzzle over this new experience. The situation intrigues me more than it concerns me. I have never breathed volcanic air before, so I have no idea of its effect. Surrendering to the inevitable, I scan the area for a comfortable place to rest and await the results. I choose an outcropping of rock that will work as a backrest.

Our ice dome is not far from the base of Mount St. Helens. Close enough for the inventors; the engineers of our city, to pipe heat into our small community, but far enough to protect us from the eruptions that ravage the mountain. The proximity to the active volcano and vented gasses means the air is un-breathable. Near the base of St. Helens, I've also seen similar rivers of melted lava much like the ribbon of red downhill from me.

I close my eyes and draw long, cleansing breaths of filtered air. I am still wary of the unprotected breath I took and half expect to fall violently ill or perhaps die. Leaning my head against the rock, my eyelids grow heavy from fatigue and I fall into a troubled sleep.

*****

Several hours later, the pain in my arm and a growling stomach pull me awake.

The breath of air didn't kill me after all. Do I risk removing my visor so I can eat, or am I pushing my luck? I am too tired to move around yet. I contemplate my decision and give in to my stomach's demands. Grabbing a food pouch, I prepare myself to once more test the air quality. I carefully map out my movements conceding that not being able to use my injured arm will restrict my motion. I plan accordingly.

The food pouch rests within easy reach and I prepare to swing open my visor and tear the envelope with my teeth, when a thought occurs to me. I rethink my plan, wondering if I should refrain from eating for now and instead adjust the filter in my helmet to a lower setting to allow the cavern air to mix with my suit's filtered air? My stomach growls, but I push aside my hunger, deciding that if there are no ill side effects after my experiment, I will remove my visor while I eat my meal.

I set the food to the side and adjust the filters, then tentatively breathe in the mixture. Slipping the journal from my pocket, I take a cursory look at its condition, thankful the paper was not damaged in my fall. The screen lights ups as I press the button. Ignoring the growling in my stomach, I concentrate on reading a few pages. Losing myself in the diary's words will take the edge off my experiment. Sliding a gloved hand across the thin screen, the words materialize.

Chapter 5

I'm Not Alone

January 23, 2046

In a meeting among the senior officers, we find ourselves left with no choice but to gather our decimated troops and retreat south. The decision is to abandon this post and reinforce the squadrons protecting the Bakken oil reserves in Northern Dakota. The ever-expanding Climate army has begun to overrun our positions in Northern Alberta. The environmentalists roam the province, recruiting bodies with promises of food for the starving and fuel for heat to stave off the months of winter cold. A majority of the population in this area is without both these staples and are swelling the ranks of the Prophet's armies in exchange for these necessities.

This winter is extremely harsh, and stories bombard us daily of families dying from the lack of accessible food or perishing in fires as they desperately seek warmth from the deadly winter. Asphyxiation and loss of life from fires flaring out of control in confined, unsafe shelters are killing more people than the war.

I honestly can't say I blame civilians for choosing the side of the Climate Prophets. They are the ones controlling the majority of fuel reserves now, and can at least offer the desperate families some semblance of hope. Against overwhelming odds, we find that our government forces are steadily retreating these days and the small amounts of oil we are fighting to preserve are sadly not enough to help even a fraction of the people.

January 30, 2046

For the past week, our men have been loading and fuelling up our transport vehicles in the dead of night to avoid prying eyes. The plan is to drive our convoy of vehicles out before dawn tomorrow morning, and try to slip away from this posting and travel to North Dakota.

The forecast for tomorrow calls for severe blizzard conditions, which I hope will mask our retreat. Most of the Climate army's troops have little, if any winter gear. The cold and snow will work in our favour. The big four-wheel drive transports will lead the way, breaking trail through the snowdrifts that cover the roads. The drive on the winter roads will be arduous; there is no extra fuel to waste on road clearing.

Sergeant Griffins came to talk to me earlier this evening. He has been away from our camp for the past few days on a scouting mission. He explained that conditions away from our camp are desperate. Small towns have become overrun with transients seeking shelter from the cold. The wooden structures in these communities have disappeared, the material stripped from the houses and repurposed for cooking and warmth.

The word is that centres all through the north are organizing caravans of men and horse drawn wagons to venture into the receding forests for the precious commodity they contain. Communities have begun hoarding the wood against the remainder of the cold months, pitting town against town for the rapidly depleting source of fuel. I don't envy these people. The northern winters are brutal at best, and by all accounts this one is shaping up to be colder than average. I fear that within the month, this particular community will be cut off from help if the heavy snowfalls persist. May they all be successful in surviving until spring?

January 31, 2046

As we leave Fort McMurray, I look about, disheartened. When we first arrived at this posting, the forests crowded the highways, and the trees had licked at the edges of the small towns along the route. In the shine of the truck's headlights, all that is visible are barren fields leading away from the highway in unbroken blankets of snow, with the odd tree stump poking above the white layers. Moonlight casts shadows across spindly stalks of willows standing desolate where once was a healthy forest. Trails crisscross the snowy landscape, pounded into the frozen earth by townsfolk as they voyage further and further for a supply of wood.

The next town south is a graveyard of concrete foundations. The building materials stripped from the houses leave only brick or steel structures standing for shelter. These serve as community centres where large fires burn around the clock. As we leave the North, I find my thoughts troubled by the unfortunate amount of casualties caused by the onslaught of frigid temperatures. With the persistent cold spell the water supplies are beginning to freeze. The Northern part of the province is proving deadly for the locals.

February 5, 2046

We have been pushing south for almost a week. The going is slow. We are often forced to stop and walk ahead of the convoy with shovels to clear a lane on the highway. Even the largest, heaviest trucks in our train have become stuck breaking a trail through the drifted snow that blocks the roads. Each man in our unit takes turns wielding shovels, myself included.

As the week draws on, every man collapses from fatigue at the end of our drives. Hours are wasted every day while we fight the winter conditions and the lack of sleep brought on by the extreme cold only adds to our problems. We can't even spare the extra fuel to leave the trucks running at night to warm ourselves. I am having doubts as to whether we will make the long journey to Minot, North Dakota.

February 6, 2046

We have stopped for the evening just off the highway near the city of Lethbridge, in southeastern Alberta, only a couple hours north of the U.S. border. The city sits on top of a river valley and was regarded as a bastion of activity on the open prairie.

This part of the province had very little in the way of trees to begin with, and the small supply disappeared quickly. We had heard that the majority of people who once called this city home migrated west, joining the massive exodus to the mountains. The Rocky Mountains provide shelter in the way of mountain caves, animals for food an abundance of trees for fires.

One thing I've noticed on our trek from the north is the vast open spaces. Areas that were a short time ago covered with farmhouses, barns and wind belts and surrounded by green flowing fields of grain lay in the winter snow, stripped and deserted. The odd pile of scrap and abandoned foundations stand like grave markers on the dead farms. The wind is ceaseless now as it blows down from the mountains and across vast tracts of open land.

February 7, 2046

I am sitting down to write a few words before our camp is broken down and loaded into the trucks. It's a crisp morning, and the sun is just starting to rise; the sky is clear. The day promises to be cold. Ice crystals dance in the air and glitter in the first light of day.

The calm is broken by gunshots. Our scouts reported they had not seen anyone in this area when we stopped last night, but now I can hear the sentries scrambling. The men are calling to each other...

Back in the cavern, I power down the reading page. The mixture of air I'm breathing is making me a little dizzy, but overall I feel fine. I grab a couple of food pouches and remove my visor. The grumbling in my stomach exceeds my need to be cautious. The food has little taste, but it serves its purpose. I consume my meal while I keep casting my eyes about, growing familiar with the area. I escaped the deadly temperatures on the surface, and I was damn lucky not to die from the fall, so I resolve to be more vigilant, especially since I don't know what lies ahead down in this cavern.

Placing my rations in my pack, I secure my visor tight to my helmet and stand up, looking for banks of snow that I can melt down for drinking water. My eyes follow the hill upward, away from the lava flow. Rocks of all sizes litter the rising slope and meld into the background where the light from the river and the darkness of the cave become one. At about that line, I spot tinges of lighter ground cover. I walk uphill. The area under my feet is still spongy, but as I increase the distance from the river, the footing grows firmer while the temperature drops rapidly.

Clambering over mounds of earth and boulders, I walk uphill, my back to the heat thrown off by the lava flow. The light from the river fades to dark. A pile of boulders blocks my path. As I begin to wind my way around the rocks, a familiar and surprising sound breaks the silence. I stop in my tracks. Behind the cover of boulders, I stand and listen. I hear people talking.

Crouching in the shadows, I slowly inch my head forward. The cavern opens wide in front of me. I search the area near the boulders, then raise my head, methodically sweeping the horizon. Slowly my eyesight adjusts to the darkness. Scattered piles of tumbled rock soon become distinguishable. All is still, but I continue peering into the dark for the source of the voices, my eyes narrowed, my sight strained as I concentrate on the shadows.

I pick out the faintest outline of a trail as it snakes across the ground and I trace the path with my eyes until it disappears in the dark void. At the edge of my vision, I see a slip of movement, then another. I hold my breath in anticipation and lean closer to the rocks. Is the cavern air playing a trick on my mind or… mesmerized I watch as two silhouettes walk among the field of scattered rocks.

Chapter 6

First Contact

The drink I started out for all is but forgotten, as I remain tight to the rocks and stare dumbfounded, tracking the moving shadows. Curiosity and excitement win over my sense of caution at the discovery of other individuals in this buried cavern. I am too far from the New Capital for these people to be of my city, or so I believe. So many questions are raised. I always assumed that settlements other than ours existed, but have never found evidence to prove my assumptions.

Slowly making my way around the boulders, I scan the open ground between where I wait and the path the pair is walking. I can't see much in the way of cover, no darker objects protruding in this poorly lit section of the cavern. There are no piles of rock large enough for me to hide behind as I track the two. My visor amplifies the failing light from the distant river. The outlines are faint and they flit in and out of view, depending on the depth of darkness.

I warn myself to move carefully. There is no way for me to judge how well these strangers see in the cavern, or if their eyesight is better than mine. I wait beside the rocks as the distance between us increases. When the silhouettes reach the limits of the illumination of my visor, I slip from cover and thread my way over the trail.

The path weaves in and out, around and then straight, skirting small piles and then larger boulders created by old lava flows. A few times, I stumble and trip over loose rocks strewn across the trail. My breathing increases from exertion and the unexpectedness of discovering the cavern's inhabitants. With each new breath, a metallic taste layers my mouth, and each time I inhale, my lungs burn from the ash-laden air. Switching my air supply back to the suit's filters, I sit and wait for the air inside my helmet to refresh.

Within minutes, the burning sensation eases. I climb to my feet, ready to resume my pursuit, but find I have lost sight of them in the shadows. Now, once again, I question whether I really had seen some one out there or if the tainted air of the cavern is causing me to hallucinate.

I stand and look around. No. I am positive that I saw movement in the shadows and the silhouettes are real. They have to be. How else would I have found this trail worn through the lava field? Moving forward, I continue picking my way along the uneven path. I put more emphasis on watching the trail for tripping hazards while I hurry forward than checking ahead for the others.

Two trains of thought bombard me. Could the outlines I glimpsed be some of my missing colleagues? Perhaps they, too, inadvertently stumbled across this cavern and are trapped with no way to return to the surface and home to the New Capital or...the other thought both intrigues and at the same time frightens me. The thought of other secluded settlements existing outside our small community and could I have possibly fallen into one.

Will the people be friendly and accepting when we meet or...?

The trail winds back, closer to the river of lava, and then follows a parallel course. With the enhancement from my visor, the river's glow brightens the cave's surroundings: the path grows clearer. I lift my head. My strides lengthen. The footing is better than further back on the trail, the path widens.

I pull up. Ahead in the light are the two figures I saw earlier. A flash of their clothing betrays their position as they walk around a bend and disappear, my line of sight blocked by a tangle of rocks. I pick up my pace. Carelessness replaces caution with each step as I hurry to keep the pair in sight.

Rushing to make the bend, I stumble as loose debris rolls under my foot. Quickly climbing to my feet, I scramble over the last bit of trail to reach the pile of rocks and look around. The pair is no longer visible. I put my arm up and lean against the pile letting my breath catch up with me.

Damn. I'm obviously not very good at this type of thing. I've never had to track anyone before. Very few people ventured up to the surface, and our ice dome isn't large enough for somebody to hide for long.

I stop the self-recrimination. I decide I have to keep to this path because logic tells me it must lead somewhere. I should be able to find out where the two are heading. This will give me time to study the area and possibly allow me to determine if the people are friendly. With their help perhaps I can return to the surface.

My throat is dry. I had forgotten yet again to find some water. I gaze ahead at the trail then upward away from the lava flow fixing landmarks in my mind that will allow me to relocate this path once I satisfy my thirst.

Confident I can find my way back, I skirt the boulders that block my way. I will have to leave the trail and distance myself from the heat of the red river in order to find ice to melt. With my throat parched, I leave the shelter of the boulders and I take a step onto the path circling the outcropping. I walk around the corner.

My heart jumps, and my eyes go wide. There, not 10 feet away from me, stand the people I was following. They wait tight to the backside of the rocks, watching me round the corner. I stare at them, they stare at me, nobody moves.

Their suits are different from the one I wear. A camouflage pattern and flowing, almost like...a robe? I have never seen this type of clothing before, but for some reason, they seem eerily familiar.

"Hi," I stutter. "My name is Mike." I remain frozen in my tracks, not knowing what else to do. The strangers stand motionless, looking me over. I can make out the features of their faces through the hooded visors covering their heads. One man, one woman, neither looks pleased to see me.

In a monotone voice, the man asks. "How did you find this place? Where did you come from?"

My voice fails as I try to get the words out. "I...I fell through an opening in the ice from the surface." I finally manage to spit out. The look on their faces tells me that they are having trouble with my explanation.

The man pulls a gun from under his robe and motions me forward. I throw my good arm in the air to calm the situation.

"Whoa, wait a minute," I shout. "I am lost like you two. I am not armed, nor am I here to harm anyone."

The gun in the man's hand does not waver. Not so friendly, I guess. I turn my head to look farther down the path, then back at the robed figures. With a more threatening gesture of the gun, the man motions me to walk.

Now, what am I going to do? I have one injured arm and no weapon to fight my way out of this. I start walking, acutely aware of the crunch of footsteps on the trail from the two following behind. Slowly, deliberately, I place one foot in front of the other, my mind a mixture of conflicting thoughts. The sight of the robes troubles me for some reason. More so than the fact that I am being ushered down an unknown path at gunpoint.

We walk onward. I stop suddenly. The robes. But can it be? Details from the written pages of the diary rush into my head. There was a faction that used to wear clothing like these two, but this group was thought to have disappeared near the end of the Climate Wars. The leaders of this movement blamed for the ruin of civilization. They were the ones known as the Climate Prophets

But that can't be. The prophets and their followers were hunted: the Eco-terrorists were treated as pariahs and jailed or killed until they were believed extinguished. The Climate army's war on fossil fuels unleashed an era of renewable energy sources that led to the earth violently shaking and the beginning of the end.

Earthquake activity increased, decades of unprecedented volcanic eruptions rocked the planet and the skies filled with toxic ash clouds and the end of the sun. As the Climate armies fought their way across the globe, they left behind fields of massive turbines to replace the energy lost from oil production for the energy-starved world

When the burning of fossil fuels became prohibited and the Prophet's armies destroyed the world's oil supplies, more and more turbines were needed. As the decades passed, acres upon acres of the metal skeletons reached high into the sky, heavy blades driven by the winds, turning and shaking, the towers replacing forests of trees and crowding the landscape.

The output of the turbines failed to satisfy world consumption, so millions of holes were bored deep into the planet to take advantage of the thermal heat buried deep underground. This weakened the earth's foundation further. Then the unthinkable happened. The vibrations and the weakened bedrock had fatal consequences. The earth trembled.

By the time scientists realized the cost of this mistake, time had run out to reverse the looming catastrophe. A few small flare-ups at first, but as the earth continued to tremble more volcanoes became active. Volcanoes that hadn't vented in millennia now poured lava and spat plumes of dust skyward. With the eruptions and the lava came the ash and slowly over time, the build-up of clouds choked out the sun.

I can't recall all the details, but I don't think that the sun has shone through the dust clouds for almost 150 years. No sun, no heat and worse of all, no crops for food. The earth cooled, and the current ice age began.

A rough hand on my back urges me forward, ending my reverie. Keeping my head down, I walk on still, puzzling over the robes the two are wearing. If my assumptions are correct, will the leaders of this community be any more receptive to my presence then the man with the gun?

The excitement of discovering a hidden civilization changes to fear and warnings creep into my head. If these people are ancestors of the Climate Prophets' and they've kept themselves hidden this long…what are the chances that I will be able to leave…or even remain alive?

Chapter 7

Hostile Environment

The farther we walk, the brighter the cavern becomes. My visor's not equipped to handle light of this magnitude. The optics were designed to enhance the weak gloom on the surface, not to diffuse the glare of powerful lights.

Outlines of buildings appear on the horizon. My eyes burn from the intensity of light. I find I can't turn away...I can't stop staring...the sight is...unbelievable.

Worries of being captured and the man with the gun pointed at my back fade to feelings of awe as the manifestation of the city rises before my eyes and buildings take on form with each step closer. Actual buildings, just like the ones my grandfather would describe in his stories. Not caves of rock and ice like my home in the New Capital, but metal structures.

It appears to be the same type of shiny metal material once used in the construction of the wind turbines, with their massive blades that lay buried beneath layers of ice and snow. Occasionally, the raging winds uncover these behemoths, but those discoveries are few and far between. Obviously, that is not the case down here.

I slow to a shuffle. The approaching sight is beyond my wildest imagination. From the distance, the buildings look incredible and as we walk closer, I start to wonder if I hadn't died in the fall through the cracked ice and perhaps this is heaven.

A hand strikes my back, reminding me that I'm neither dead nor dreaming. Then a second more forceful shove urges me forward. I stumble a few steps before regaining my footing. The amazement of seeing this spectacular city rise from the lava fields and the excitement it brings is jarred from my mind as the reminder of my uncertain future is forced back upon me.

Shading my eyes, I increase my stride. The trail dips downward at a slow but steady incline before cutting back between large towering rocks. The view of the city passes from sight as the path winds back and forth, skirting the scattered boulders formed by cooled lava. The cascade of bright light illuminates our way.

Winding around more rocks that bend the trail, the metal buildings and surrounding area slowly start to materialize once more. They now become much clearer and larger as each footstep brings me closer to this hidden wonder.

Small clusters of people are gathering at the edge of the city. With each step, the buildings and faces of the onlookers in the brightly lit city fill the horizon. I gaze straight ahead, absorbing the many fascinating details of the growing city and the strange people awaiting our arrival.

Without being able to help myself, I slow again, dumbstruck at the sights and sounds looming at the end of the path. The whispers of the crowd's voices drift over the trail to my ears. People walking from all directions join the gathering that has all ready collected, increasing the size of the crowd.

I notice the people are wearing similar robes as the pair behind me, but in a variety of colours, some with sashes, some without. It takes me a while to realize that these people are not wearing helmets or any visible type of breathing apparatus, unlike my captors.

Could it be possible? Is the air in the city clean enough to breathe without the aid of filters and the temperature warm enough for inhabitants to move freely without thermal devices? Or, are these people different, immune to the fumes released by the lava. Are the volcano gases not toxic to them?

I think back several hours. Didn't I also experiment with the air quality once I discovered that my feeding tube broke in the fall? Do I dare shut off my suit's air scrubber? I quickly shelf that idea and decide against it. Probably not the time to experiment with my breathing until I find out what is in store for me. I should know soon. I am only yards away from the crowds of the glimmering city.

I take a chance and look from one side to the other. We have apparently not travelled a great distance from the river of lava since I don't see signs of packed ice close by. Looking up, the height of this cavern is staggering; the brilliant light of the city is not able to penetrate the darkness at the upper reaches of the dome.

I am now close enough to make out the faces of the crowd awaiting our approach. All the faces carry the same blank look, but some I can tell have a tinge of fear hidden behind their eyes. Everyone is staring at me like I am some strange entity, unlike anything they have ever seen. Why? Am I not the same species as these strangers? Have they never seen anyone other than their neighbours?

"Stop," a voice behind me commands. I quit walking and return the awkward glances of the crowd. As much as I want to look up at the shiny city behind the crowd, I am unable to raise my eyes. I hear murmurs, but everyone is standing still, quietly talking in their little groups and some point in my direction. Unfazed, I stare right back at them.

Then in the rear of the now-sizeable crowd, people shift apart. Men and women move to the side, clearing a path for a handful of colourfully robed elderly men to pass. Behind the old men follows another group, three more bodies dressed in camouflage robes matching the two people behind me. These three have guns slung over their shoulders. My heart races with the unknown.

The elderly men are dressed alike in bright green robes. They stop a few steps away, the soldiers a step behind them. The old men study me suspiciously, and then look at each other.

"Who are you?" one of the older men asks. "Where are you from?"

"Mike…my name is…" I start to answer, but one of the old men motions with his hand to silence me.

"You will have time to answer our questions later. Take this criminal to the cages," the man commands the soldiers behind him.

"Hey! I…" I start to protest. The two soldiers who led me to the city secure my arms and join the three that accompanied the old men. They lead me into the path of the milling crowd. People glare at me, uncertain, while I am marched away to who knows where.

The hands of the guards are firm on my arms; the other soldiers follow tight behind. What have I fallen into? I wonder. Nobody here seems friendly. I notice signs of loathing and hatred hidden in the faces of the curious bystanders who maintain eye contact.

I try to catch glimpses of the city as I am escorted to wherever and whatever our destination. Obviously, these people can see that I am not a threat. From the looks of this strange crowd and the bright, shiny city, they must know by my attire that their technology is better than anything I would have.

Our journey takes us past a window. My reflection is almost unrecognizable. Suddenly, I understand the hostility of these strangers. In the reflection, my suit is covered from head to toe in a dirty black substance, the mud from by the river where I fell. I want to laugh and shout that I am not a monster although at the moment I must certainly look like one.

The journey into the city doesn't last long. The soldiers stop just inside the lava fields. One of the soldiers rushes in front and opens a door to a low-lying building. I resist going inside, but the guards quickly overpower me.

Lights flicker on and I see cages, rows and rows of cages. I am dragged to one nearest the entrance and watch, as the cage door is pulled open. The two men thrust me through the opening. By the time I regain my balance, I hear the metal door clang shut.

"Stop. You don't understand," I shout at the backs of the retreating soldiers, but they are already walking outside, leaving me alone in this room filled with cages. The door swings shut and I stand close to the bars, my eyes fixed on the closed door. Now what?

I test the bars of the cell, steel firm and round and only wide enough for my hand to pass through. The lights in the room dim with the closing of the door, but with the help of my visor, I have little trouble seeing the confines of my cage. A shelf off the far wall I presume is a bed, there's a hole in the floor and then plenty of round metal bars.

I wander over to the shelf and sit down. My throat is scratchy and dry. This reminds me of the ice I had set out to find when I met the two on the trail. I forgot how thirsty I was amid all the excitement.

"Can I get a drink of water?" I yell. The echo of my voice in the room is the only answer. I hang my head in despair, feeling sorry for myself.

I don't know how long I sit like this before I hear a voice.

"They are going to do away with you...you know?" a quiet female voice announces. I jump to my feet and walk the few short steps to the front of the cage. With my hands wrapping around the bars, I turn my head trying to get a glimpse of the person speaking. Straining to see toward the far end of the room, I gaze unblinking into the dim light.

Slowly out of the shadows, a young woman walks toward the cage, her hands holding a tray in front of her. She steps into sight, a drab brown robe draped over her shoulders and her arms jutting out from a part at the front of her gown. I study her face. Even in the shade of her hood, I can see she's pretty. Strands of brown hair spill out of the neckline of her robe.

"Who are you?" It is my turn to ask questions.

The girl stops in front of the bars and looks up at me through a pair of light green eyes, her gaze nervous and darting. Through a slot in the bars, she passes me the tray and then a jug. I place the tray down before accepting the pitcher. I stand with the container in my hand looking down into her face.

"What do you mean…do away with me? Who are you, what is this place called?" I desperately ask her in my search for answers.

"They will do away with you like they did away with all the others," she repeats as she backs away from the cage. Then, without another word she disappears back down the hallway and into the dark from where she came.

Chapter 8

Understanding

I gaze into the dark long after she disappears, my visor pressed tight to the bars, the jug in my arm all but forgotten as I try to decipher the girl's warning. Who would do away with me? The old men running the city, the guards, who?

And what did she mean by the others? What others? Were there a lot of people locked in these cages before me?

The weight of the water jug pulls my thoughts back to the cell. I walk over to the metal shelf and set the water down, then return and lift the tray of food from the floor. I place it next to the water and sit beside it. Ever since the meeting in the cavern, I have been puzzled, discovering these foreign people and a shiny city, the old men in robes and the girl who brought my food. I sit contemplating the events of the last few hours. I don't know what to think about it all.

First, I am swept off my ice sled, then the fall through the ice cavity to the bottom of this cavern. If all of that and the discovery of the strangers on the path wasn't enough, now I find myself locked up in a cage, awaiting an uncertain future.

I take stock of my possessions. I don't have much. My pack lays somewhere miles back in the cavern. I set it down on my search for water, and then forgot it when I saw the shadows on the path. All I have remaining is my reading paper and my thermal suit. Not much to aid an escape.

I remove my helmet absently rubbing the mud caked to the outside. Working it clean I next think of my suit and check the charge before powering down to save the batteries. I have a feeling it will be needed when I take my leave of this place. The ominous warning by the woman resonates through the darkness of the room, and I have no plans to accept their deadly fate.

The tray contains solid nourishment of some sort, vegetables like the ones grown in our greenhouses. A rubbery slab of brown and next to it a white square, soft in the middle with crusty edges. I pick the strange brown slab and find I have to bite quite hard to tear a chunk free. It has a unique texture, chewy and unlike anything I've eaten. I pick at the rest of the food while I sit in the dark.

The meal is good and quite different than the packets of powdered food of my home. Sampling the items, I can't help wonder what it's like to live in this shiny city. There is plenty of food and people can walk about freely without the constraints of a helmet to filter the air and the needed warmth of a heat suit.

Paradise, I realize. It is too bad I have arrived under such hostile conditions. I empty the plate and drink from the flask before settling back waiting for whatever comes next.

With my back propped against the wall, I fight to remain vigilant. The combined warmth of the room and the food makes me sleepy and I doze off.

*****

The creak of a door opening and male voices stirs me from my slumber. The room's lights flicker to life. Blinking the sleep from my eyes, it takes me a few heartbeats to recall where I am. Voices travel from the doorway and the group of old men gathers at the bars of my cage, inspecting me.

"Why have you come here? How did you find us?" One of the elders asks. "Who sent you?"

"I fell through the ice from the surface." I explain. "No one sent me because we never knew people lived down here let alone that such a city could even exist. If I hadn't fallen into the cavern, never in a lifetime would I have guessed that a whole civilization lived beneath the ice." My answer is greeted with looks of disbelief and I study the men while they glance at each other.

"My name is Mike Ryan. I am an ice racer. I come from the New Capital, a long way from here, located at the base of Mount St. Helens." I talk quickly, hoping to convince them that what I say is the truth.

The men turn away and talk quietly with each other. They face back to the cell and continue watching me like I'm... an animal in a cage.

"We will be back later. We know that you have been sent to spy on our city. When next we talk, you will confess to the truth," the spokesman for the group says, as they turn to leave. When the door latches closed and the lights go down, I find myself standing in the dark alone with my thoughts once more. I need a way out of this prison, and I need it soon.

The morning passes. From the far end of the row of cages, a second door squeals on its hinges as it opens. A sliver of light sneaks in from the opening and stretches across the floor. Soft footsteps resonate on the hard floor and follow the light approaching my cell. The same girl from the previous day walks toward me, another tray in her hands. She stops short of my cage and raises her head to look at me. She hesitates, wary that I'm standing close to the bars. Backing away, I talk to her.

"What is your name? What did you mean last night when you said they would do away with me?"

She slides the food through the slot and waits for me to grab it, then backs away and with her head motions to the used tray sitting on the shelf. I quickly exchange the containers and slide the empty one back through the slot.

"Annaliese." She replies then lowers her eyes to the ground.

"Where are we, Annaliese?" I ask, trying desperately to start a conversation. She remains quiet and I can see she's scared. "What is this place?" I try again.

"Our home is called Adams Mountain." She very softly answers without raising her head. "You're not here to spy on us like the others, are you? If you were free would you return with your soldiers and attack us?" Her voice trembles as she asks the questions. "The Prophets tell us that is why you are here."

"The Climate Prophets?" I ask, not certain that I had heard her correctly.

She startles and backs farther way from the cage. "Then it is true what they say. You are going to attack us, aren't you?" She says. "How else would you know about the prophets?"

"No...no, I..." I scramble to pull my reading paper out of my suit and power it up. Quickly scanning the entries, I find one that will help me explain and turn the page toward her. "Do you read?" I say as I show her the article. She looks at me like I had just grown a third eye.

"Doesn't everybody?" She replies. I have no answer for this because in the New Capital, reading material is very scarce and learning to read is not a luxury many want or bother to do.

"Ah. Yeah. Sure. I just thought..." I didn't know what to say. Remembering the paper, I shove it toward her. "I only know about the Climate Prophets because of my grandfather's diary." I wave the paper hoping she understands. "Who has been attacking you?"

"No one...not yet," Annaliese replies and I study her face while she thinks about my question before looking me in the eyes. "The prophets are very vigilant in their protection of the city." She says this defiantly, my question obviously bothering her. "Whenever intruders are caught lurking in the area, they are captured and held in these cages. The prophets insist that this practice is vital to our survival. They warn that outsiders only seek us out to bring harm to our people and to steal our resources."

"Does this happen often," I ask. "Where are the others who've been captured?"

"Prisoners remain in the cages for a long time. The Prophets try them before a council and then once condemned, they are confined to the oil pits." She pauses, troubled. "Once they are sentenced, they can never leave, they are never allowed to return to where they came from." She speaks these words with an underlying sadness.

The word oil catches my attention. "Oil. There hasn't been oil for centuries. Its use was outlawed during the Climate Wars," I say sceptically, my hand tapping the reading paper.

Maybe I grew yet another eye judging from the way she looks at me.

"What do you think powers this city, the lights and the heat, the massive purifiers that rid the air of toxins and the pumps that circulate fresh air from the surface, all the equipment? Where are you from?" she asks.

I was aware of the constant humming and vibrations, but hadn't given them much thought. Of course, machines power the city. I am enthralled with the concept. Nobody at the New Capital would imagine this was possible. We have a few very crude generators but the small amounts of fuel we scavenge barely keep them running. They are used to power the buildings that grow our food or incubators for newborn babies.

A thousand questions rush through my brain and I trip over my words as they leave my mouth. The girl, Annaliese, looks scared and backs away from my cage.

"I have said too much." Her quiet voice is muted by her retreating footsteps. "I will be back with your supper."

With the bars grasped in my hands and my face pressed tightly against the metal, I call after her. Her footsteps fade into the darkness.

Chapter 9

A Friendly Face

I peer into the darkness long after Annaliese has disappeared. A bout of despair is brought on by the silence of the room. What can I do, how can I leave when I can't even get out of this cage?

Shoving away from the bars I dejectedly pace back and forth before stopping at the steel shelf and sit down, the tray of food pushed aside, ignored. Sitting hunched over, my head cupped in my hands, I stare unblinkingly at the floor, ready to surrender to whatever awaits.

Then with each new breath, the bleakness starts to recede. Sitting up straight, I fill my lungs with courage and my mood begins to lighten, my determination grows. I have faced far greater dangers every time I ventured on to the unforgiving surface of this miserable planet while piloting the ice sled. A mistake there meant certain death, but locked in this cage and being held captive by a tangible enemy allowed me a reasonable chance of escape.

I rethink my circumstances. In the cage, I have little. But once outside these barred walls, the environment is warm, and the air is breathable. Outside of the building are thousands of people and a whole city of wonder; surely there is something I can use, some tools or weapons to aid in my flight.

I stand up and start pacing again, trying to recall everything I noticed on my short walk to this building. The crowds of people, the tall shiny buildings behind them, guards with guns... but maybe somewhere in all of that, a way out.

Annaliese mentioned something about air being drawn from the surface, which means there has to be a route from the city and a way out of here. She had also told me this place is called Adams Mountain. From my limited knowledge of geography, I am aware that Adams Mountain is less than 40 miles from the base of Mount St. Helens.

I think about this. Forty miles doesn't seem that far, but on the surface when fighting against constant blizzards and minus 70-degree temperatures even with my thermal suit, walking the 40 miles would be nearly impossible. Without the ability to recharge the batteries that power my suit, I wouldn't last more than a couple of days. My backpack and shovel lay forgotten back on the trail, and I don't think I will have time to retrieve them.

The afternoon passes slowly while I plan my escape. A shuffling at the far end of the room morphs into footsteps. The thought of Annaliese returning boosts my spirits. I glance at the uneaten food she had brought me earlier. Grabbing the tray, I walk the short distance to the bars, ready for the exchange.

I breathe a sigh of relief when Annaliese materializes from the shadows carrying a new meal. I stand away from the bars as she slides the food through the opening. Grabbing the tray with one hand, I slip the uneaten meal back to her.

"Is there something wrong with the food?" Her voice is laden with concern.

"Um…no, I am sure it is fine. I don't have much of an appetite, I guess, with the worry of what is going to happen to me." I lie and feel awful for fibbing. I can't exactly tell her that I forgot about the food because I was plotting my escape.

She lifts her head. Her eyes search my face, before glancing back at the floor

"They are to discuss you in council tomorrow," she says quietly. "Soon after that, I am sure that they will do away with you…I'm sorry." The words whisper past her lips.

"I don't want to die yet, especially here in a strange city," I stammer. A flash of anger takes hold of me. "No. I will not die here."

"I am sorry," she apologizes again, and watches me from the other side of the bars.

"You don't have to apologize," I console her. "This isn't your fault." Not relishing the thought of being left alone, I ask; "Can you stay and talk for a while?" She doesn't answer. She continues to stand outside the cage; the tray clasped in her hands.

"What do you do here?" I ramble on, hoping she will hang around.

"Not too much," she reluctantly answers. "My father is one of the Prophets, so I am free to roam the city. When I saw the guards lock you up, I arranged to deliver your meals."

"Well, thanks, I guess. What's it like living here?" I quickly fumble for another question in order to keep her talking. "Are you happy here? What do you do with your time?"

She tells me how she wanders the city helping out where ever she can and about the day-to-day workings of the Adams Mountain, a tone of sadness in her voice. Changing the subject, she asks me about the place I call home.

I tell her about the giant ice caves at the bottom of Mount St. Helens where my people struggle to survive and how I am an Ice Racer. The conversation helps me temporarily forget about my captivity. I describe my ice sled and explain how the majority of my time is spent on the ice and snow above ground and how my crew and I explore and transport supplies of oil and scavenged materials back to the New Capital.

I tell her how lucky she is to be living in such a city that has power and heat, and I presume ample amounts of food judging from the trays she has served me. Food that is much better than what we eat back at the Capital. I explain how the food we eat is comprised of moss that is harvested from along the rivers of lava. It is mixed with crops grown in our greenhouses. With a limited amount of energy to heat and light the indoor gardens, the quantities produced are less than the hunger of our people.

"I would offer you a chair," I say in the way of lightening the conversation and waved my arm in a sweeping motion around the cell. For an instant, the corners of her mouth lift in what is almost a smile.

"I'm good." She responds. "You told me about a reading paper…would you mind if I looked at it?"

I hesitate. The paper is my most prized possession, and I jealously guard it.

"You said something about writings concerning the Prophets. How far back in time does this paper go?" She stops. "The history accepted by the Prophets dates back to the founding of this city, nothing before that. It is the prophet's law. We are taught that recordings of history before this city was founded are blasphemous and contain fabricated untruths denigrating the plight of our people."

I slip the paper out of my suit. I study her as debate rages inside my head. I decide to trust her and shove the thin document through the opening in the bars. She sets the tray of cold food on the floor and apprehensively accepts my offering.

"There is a button on the bottom to turn the power on," I instruct. She presses her thumb over the button and holds it until the words on the paper light up. I remain silent as she swipes through the pages. Her eyes grow bigger with excitement as she reads the dates of the diary entries.

"Did these things actually happen?" She asks after reading random paragraphs. Her eyes remain glued on the paper. I tell her a brief family history and how the diary began during the Climate Wars and how the paper was passed down from relative to relative until my grandfather, and then finally to me.

"I have never doubted the written words, but I can't imagine people inventing things to write in a diary. The history we were taught in school and the stories of our elders match the writings," I add. I explain to her who the elders are and how we rely on their recollection of the past because of the lack of written material. All our teachings are passed on and memorized, from one generation to the next. There was no other way.

I think carefully about my next words and then gulp before speaking. "Why don't you take the paper with you and read it. If I'm to be done away with by the Prophets, I would rather you hold on to the reading paper than it be lost or destroyed." I say the last words with as much bravado as I can, so she won't worry.

Concealing the paper under her robe, Annaliese bends down to pick up the food tray and turns to walk away.

"Don't give up hope just yet." I hear her whisper before her footsteps retreat into the darkness at the end of the building.

Chapter 10

A Disturbing Reality and Hope

Annaliese left the young Ice Racer and walked passed the row of cages exiting into an adjoining building. The reading paper the inmate gave her secretly hidden in the folds of her robe, her excitement barely contained. She returned the tray to the building's cooking area, finished her chores and raced to the privacy of her room in what the townsfolk secretly referred to as the palace.

Her father's house wasn't anything like a palace, but it was certainly grander than the other homes in the city. This perk likely came with her father being the eldest and the most revered Prophet. A reference she tried to ignore, but found hard to escape.

People were very guarded about what they said when she was around, but she occasionally overheard their whispers of discontent. Her father and the other Prophets were stringent and not at all forgiving when it came to the citizens of Adams Mountain obeying their rules.

To question the prophet's laws or beliefs was received with extreme prejudice and any outward show of defiance was treated as blasphemy. The punishment was swift and the penalties harsh. She understood and accepted this without question, but in her outings around the city, she could tell that not everyone had the same unwavering faith. Every time strangers were marched into the city, she found herself questioning the strict system.

One time when she was a child, she foolishly voiced her concerns. For this, her father sternly scolded her and warned about such dangerous thoughts. He even threatened of the consequences of rebellious thinking, but with age, the repeated and scripted explanations her father used to quell her doubts had started to sound feeble and contrite.

Annaliese knew that being the daughter of the High Prophet, she of all people should without a doubt accept the word of the Prophets. Her daily meetings with the people she considered friends and neighbours, and the fear she glimpsed behind their eyes, unsettled her. Each day spent among the people of Adams Mountain, watching them toil under the rigid laws and their quiet condemnation of the prophet's rule, tore at her soul. Not born of a rebellious nature, she found her thoughts often drifting in that direction especially more often as she began to question the status quo.

Annaliese trembled at the thought her father would find out that she had a paper containing an account of history that differed from the prophets' teachings. The written history contradicted the city archives and she was frighteningly aware of the harsh manner that had befallen other free thinkers. She could expect no different treatment, High Prophet's daughter or not.

Many of the archives at the libraries and schools contained accounts of a history that she found tainted and hard to accept. As her mind searched for clearer meanings, the explanations by the Prophets fell short of convincing her. The accounts of the Climate Prophets and history of the city were taught at a very young age. They were, to this city, the one and only truth.

Annaliese pushed these troubling thoughts from her head, rushed to her room and locked her door before tentatively sliding the reading paper out from the concealment of her robe. With her legs folded underneath, she huddled in her bedside chair and soon became engrossed in words and a history alien to what she learned as a child.

Skimming through the paper, she became shocked at what was written. Several times, she turned from the paper, appalled by the recorded events of history. But she resumed reading. The words better suited her true beliefs, not the convoluted truth she was spoon-fed since birth. Years of questioning and deductions formed her beliefs but she was still disturbed by the writings.

She paused in her reading. Annaliese had to consider that this paper might not be anything close to the truth. Could the prisoner not believe in a history that was falsely presented to him in it the same way she was forced to accept the prophets' teachings? Several times, she turned away from the diary angry and confused. The words were blasphemous, but still... did they had a certain ring of truth.

Wouldn't she be seen as being irrational by dismissing a history that ruled her life? A history that had been accepted as gospel by the entire city, in exchange for a written narration passed to her by a complete stranger, a man branded as an enemy. Weren't all outsiders who spent time in the cages here for the same purpose, to harm the citizens of Adams Mountain and cart away the resources? Wasn't that the very reason the Prophets insisted the prisoners not be allowed to leave?

Annaliese thought back to the last time that someone, other than locals whose minds were warped by heretic beliefs, occupied the cages. The timing was suspicious. These incidents began only after the rebellion in the oil mines. The guards fought for days to quell the uprising. The results left many dead, and production in the mines suffered from the depleted workforce. Of course, no one ever volunteered to work the mines.

She started questioning the prophet's tactics when their forces took to roaming the city and a surge of arrests followed. Neighbours, many whom she knew would never raise their voice to authority, were taken from their homes and families during the night and charged with crimes, many believed fabricated, against the city. The punishment was always the same. Life spent working on the floor of the mines.

The workforce slowly rebuilt, but the population grew fearful and dubious and then angered by the nature of these crimes. The fear led to a rising resentment, the fabric of the community about to tear into shreds. Annaliese remembered overhearing the worried discussions that took place at the palace. To ease the tension, the Prophets called an end to the scourge, but the shortage in the mines continued.

And then, either by miracle or an omen, the cages began to fill. A rash of enemies were captured and retained in the cells. Until the riots in the mines, the city had never faced attacks from outside forces and suddenly bands of men were apprehended lurking near the city limits. It was made to appear that all were plotting to bring death and destruction upon the people of Adams Mountain. All were proclaimed enemies and charged with crimes against society. These prisoners were sentenced to the mines and the production in the mines increased. Annaliese, however, found herself wondering at the timing. How it coincided with the needs of the Prophets? How had so many enemies suddenly found their way to her city in the cavern?

The arrest of the young ice racer, Mike Ryan, raised these suspicions once again. She found herself not thinking of him in the same light as the earlier prisoners. Or was she being foolish because she felt drawn to him for some strange reason. He seemed different than the city residents, gentle in one way, innocent in another. She had a hard time believing he came here with intentions of doing harm.

Long into the night, she read about the rise of the Climate Prophets, the Climate Wars and then the construction of the giant wind turbines and how the earth started to vibrate and shake. How, suddenly volcanoes that were dormant for hundreds of years, became active once again spewing ash and dust high into the earth's atmosphere. She read about how the skies filled with toxic clouds of dust and ash that blocked out the sun and how the planet froze.

Annaliese had never left this city; she had never walked on the surface, the Prophets forbade it. But Annaliese had heard rumours and her curiosity grew when talking with the prisoners. The same repeated stories told by different groups of captives at different times of their internment. She had heard the same repeated denials of the prophets' false charges and then the horrible accounts of life lived in subterranean communities.

Similar accounts, told by strangers unknown to each other, of the same chain of events that changed the surface of the planet until nothing more than ice and snow existed and now the written words of this diary supported those claims. The deeper into the paper she read, the more unwilling she became to accept the prophets' chronicles of history.

She initially rebuked the altered truth as desperate words by men willing to say anything to garner their release. The more she considered the bizarre tales the more she questioned her own beliefs. Now, with the written words of the reading paper, her scepticism fortified and the teachings of her father faded. The diary in her hands could well be faked, this she accepted. Still, one thing ran true; the history the Prophets presented no longer held her mind in their tight grip. Over the years too many claims by the Prophets failed to add up.

*****

Alone in my cell, I sit down to eat the food Annaliese has brought me. Each mouthful I chew with no memory of its taste, and I dwell on her parting words. Dismissing the subject, I lie down and resume plotting my escape.

If she is right and they come for me tomorrow, I will need a plan of sorts for when the cage door opens. Where they are to hold this council and how many people it involves is an unknown. I know that the more people around, the harder it will be to escape, so if I am going to break free it will have to be between this cage and the area where the meeting takes place.

How many guards will they send? The same number that escorted me to this building, I wonder? If it is indeed the same guards that brought me here, I will need to overpower them, maybe wrestle a gun away. How well trained the guards are I have no idea, but I know that the years of hard work on the ice sled had given me an unusual amount of strength. For my sake, hopefully I have enough to overpower whatever the number of guards that are sent to retrieve me.

I lay thinking, my hand turning over a spoon from the tray of food. The spoon is a light metal and bends very easily. With my fingers, I shape it this way and that until I fashion a stout point on the end. I stuff the spoon in my suit as a last resort. I can at least stab someone with it. It is the only object I have as a weapon.

The hour is growing late. I leave the metal shelf and move restlessly about the confines of my cell, my thoughts flashing between my captivity and Annaliese. I start to tire, so I sit back down. If something is to happen to me tomorrow, I don't want to spend my last hours sleeping, or so I tell myself as I struggle to keep my eyes open. Sleep eventually overcomes me.

I am woken from a troubled sleep by the sound of clanking on the cage's bars. By the time I discover where the sound originates and move to the bars, distant footsteps retreating into the darkness are all that remain. Disgusted by my tardiness, I am about to return to the metal shelf when I glance down.

On the outside of the cage, a bundle sits on the darkened floor. I bend down to examine it. Squeezing my arm through the bars, I grab the package and by twisting and pulling, I work it into my cell. When I lift up my hands to have a closer look, an object slips from the folds of cloth and rattles against the floor.

Up close, I see the bundle contains a robe. In the dim light, I can see that it is like the clothing I noticed the townsfolk wearing. I don't get it. Why would someone leave me a robe? Then I remembered the sound of clinking. Kneeling down, I slowly search for the object that fell, sliding my hand over the worn concrete, my fingertips feeling for something, anything. The light is too dim. I retrieve my visor off the shelf and look again.

Inches from my cell lay a dull thin metal object. By squeezing my arm through the bars up to my shoulder, I stretch my fingers and purposely slide them along the floor until I feel the object. With the tips of my fingers, I manoeuvre the metal closer to the cage.

I work it close enough so I can grab it with my fingers. Raising my hand to my visor, I study the object, turning it in my fingers. A strange piece of thin bent metal, one that I have not seen much of before but I know what it is. A key. I glance from my hand to the door on the cage. Maybe, just maybe this is my way out of here.

I hesitate for only a second, contemplating the key and the brown cloth and who might have left them. With a rushed urgency I pull the robe on over my suit. Curiously, I slide my hands into the robe's pockets to check for any other surprises that may be waiting.

My right-hand closes over a scrap of paper. I bring it up to my eyes and study it. A crude map is etched on the small paper.

For an instant, I think this might be a trap, but it's a chance I am willing to take. I reach my hand through the bars, the metal key held tight in my hand. Reaching and twisting I snake my arm through the bars, careful not to drop the thin metal while I move it toward the hole in the door of the cage.

With great care, I clutch the key, my heart rate quickens and sweat builds on my body.

Richard Cozicar

Drawing deep breaths to calm my nerves, I move very patiently until the key slides in the lock. Holding my breath I turn my wrist. Clunk.

Chapter 11

The Quiet Of Night

I exhale before giving the cage door a shove. It moves ever so slightly, and the hinges release a high-pitched squeal, that horrid noise only metal on metal can make. If this is a trap, I am fool enough to bite. I pull the hood of the robe over my visor and stand in the opening studying the map.

A line runs from the cage door straight down the long dark hallway of the building, the way Annaliese came and went. I am only feet from the front door of the building and a short run back into the rocky landscape that I had crossed coming to the city. I debate the door, quickly deciding against it. I turn to my left. As quietly as possible, I move in the direction traced on the map. The sounds of my footsteps ring in the still darkness.

I pass a long row of cages similar to the one that held me. The hallway seems endless as the dark gives way to the light of my visor. I feel anxious, glad to be out of the cage but apprehensive about what is to come. I keep expecting my escape to be discovered and to hear the sound of running feet chasing me.

The hallway leads past the rows of cells to a grey metal door, a sliver of light outlines the slightly open door. Creeping close, I listen for sounds of movement from the other side. As gently as I can, I push the door open ahead of me, still tense, still waiting for some alarm to announce my escape.

The lights in this section burn a little brighter and expose a room much like the one I departed. The space widens in front of me in a long, narrow chamber with shelves and lockers lining the sides. Standing in the doorway, I study the map. A line scrawled in pencil points to a doorway in the middle of this room. With more haste in my step, I hurry, ignoring the clap of my boots on the hard floor. The next door is also ajar. I pause, my fingers on the door handle, wary for any indication of a trap. The steady hum of the city generators is the only sound in the otherwise quiet night.

Overhead lights greet me as I exit the building, brighter than the prison room I was in but not awash in the bright light of the daytime when I arrived. I stop and look around. The low structure blocks my view of the streets that I had previously walked when entering the city. I find myself alone standing in a walkway between buildings. The lines on the map lead away from the city's entrance. The majority of this alley sits in shadows, undisturbed by the dim streetlights.

For the next hour, I follow the directions on the paper away from the openness of the craggy volcano rocks and deeper toward the heart of the city. The farther way from the cages I walk, the less I believe this is a setup and the more I find myself hoping that Annaliese had somehow set this process in motion.

The city is quiet. Eerily quiet other than the sound of my boots on the road and the constant drone of the machinery humming in the night. The route is littered with crates and bins, discarded boxes and other refuse piled against the walls. I dash among the stacks of cover crisscrossing the space between buildings. My pace quickens, wanting to bring this journey to an end. Approaching the opening at the end of the alley, I am about to turn the corner when a beam of light sweeps across the ground, inches from my feet.

I stop suddenly, my heart pounding in my chest, my eyes darting about for a place to hide. A few steps behind me lay a cluster of crates beside a metal bin. Two quick steps back and I squeeze into a small space between the objects. With my back pressed tight against a wall I fight the pounding in my chest, my breath frozen in my lungs. I wait.

Seconds, maybe a minute passes. Into the alley, the sound of footsteps and conversation approach. Twin beams of light travel over the dusty ground. Searching, but not whole-heartedly. My pulse pounds in my head, almost deafening me. I find that I am holding my breath, scared that the sound of my breathing will betray my presence.

The beams of light pass over again, and then the footsteps fade, signaling the light carriers are moving away from where I hide. When I can no longer hear the footfalls, I peer around the bin. The beams of light are faint and more distant. The guards at the far end of the alley wear the same type of camouflage robes like the soldiers who had marched me to the cage.

I slowly exhale and walk briskly toward the mouth of the alley. I edge close to the corner and study the street that runs past the opening. To my relief, the street is deserted, allowing me to continue following the path that was mapped out for me.

I walk and then run the remaining distance of the hand-drawn route. I calculate that I must be miles from the entrance by now, the taller buildings completely blocking any view of the way I have travelled.

My trek takes me through deserted, unfamiliar city streets. I am in another narrow, poorly lit side street. I kneel close to a wall and study the map. According to the paper, there should be a door somewhere around here. I search the walls in the dark lane. More crates and bins line either side of me, much the same as the alley behind the cage building.

Moving with deliberation, I walk close to the walls using my hands to feel the exterior in the darkened shadows for any break or outline indicating a door. I concentrate on finding an opening.

A hand touches my shoulder. I freeze, afraid to turn around. Then accepting that my short-lived freedom is over, I slide my hand under the robe and finger the bent spoon in my suit. It's the only weapon I have, but with the element of surprise, I am determined to fight my way free.

I spin, driving the spoon in my hand upwards. A grunt as the bent spoon hits flesh. My hand is knocked aside and I am thrown back into a wall. My head bounces off the wall, bright lights swim in my brain blurring my sight. I shake my head to bring my eyes into focus. A group dressed in camouflage robes surrounds me.

I tense my muscles, prepared to launch off the wall and into the group, when the guard I stabbed holds up his hand to silence me and then motions with his head for me to follow. One of his hands pressed tight to his shoulder, covering the wound left by my spoon, a dark wet patch spreading underneath his hand.

The soldiers turn their backs on me and move toward a stack of crates stacked along side a metal bin. The group members walk between the objects and begin disappearing into a doorway not easily detected unless one knew its location. The last one to cross the threshold turns and urges me to hurry. I take a couple of long strides and walk through the opening; the door swiftly bolted behind me.

Once again I am warned to remain silent and led deeper into a building, our journey stops in a small storage room. On the floor, a hatch is uncovered and pulled open, light from below exposes a set of stairs. I follow the robed people down two flights of hastily constructed stairs, slightly sturdier than a ladder. From the stairs, we pass into tunnels built beneath the city. I pause to look around at the shafts, which appear to be natural openings formed in the lava rock.

This excursion down and under the city lasts another half-hour at best, ending in a softly lit cavern the size of a small room. Standing on the opposite side of the rocky floor from where we enter is Annaliese. She looks up as I walk into the space behind my guides and our eyes meet.

Standing inside the entrance, I look over the room, confused and apprehensive. Why would Annaliese be working with the guards and why bring me here? She sees my hesitation and crosses the floor to stand in front of me. Then raising her hand, she passes my reading paper back. I study her face trying to understand what is taking place.

She smiles again and looks me in the eye. "I told you not to give up hope." As she says this, her eyes and smile reveal something else.

Chapter 12

The Explanation

"Where are we? Why are you with the guards?" Questions roll out of my mouth as I search her face for answers. Gazing down into her eyes, I wait for an explanation. Why is she working with the guards? Is this how the prisoners are done away with? Given a sliver of false hope before being hauled off for punishment, some type of game acted out for the amusement of the residents of the shiny city?

I lift my head and look away from Annaliese, my eyes roaming the interior of the room, the robed guards murmuring among themselves. The sounds of their whispered conversations radiate around me. From under their hoods, I notice furtive glances in my direction. They quickly avert their gaze when I look them in the eye.

A guard from the far end of the room strides in my direction, the others crowd around. He stops beside Annaliese, an appraising look on his face as he studies me briefly before extending his hand.

"I am Marcus," the man says as he shakes my hand. "Annaliese has told us about you. It was her idea to free you from the cages."

"I'm not sure I understand? You're guards?" I reply. "Why would you aid in my escape?"

Marcus laughs as he notices me looking at his camouflage uniform. He shrugs out of the robe and tosses it against the wall. The room goes silent, the others watching our exchange.

"Disguises," he explains. His expression turns serious. "The city is under strict curfew. When the evening comes and the lights of the city dim, no one but the night patrols are allowed outdoors and on the streets. Restrictions are in place forbidding us from leaving our homes and prohibit any group gatherings."

"So all of you are breaking the rules?" I ask suspiciously, not ready to buy into his explanation. "But what will happen when my disappearance is discovered or are you planning to return me to my cage before morning?"

I take a step back in the direction of the door and look around at the people in the room. Tensions rise while I weigh my chances of rushing the door and slipping back onto the streets of the city.

Marcus glances at Annaliese. The two exchange looks.

Marcus shrugs, "We haven't planned that far ahead yet. We've never helped anyone escape before. The other prisoners only left the cages when the council called for them and then they were marched to the oil pits to serve their sentences."

I digest this news. "Have there been a lot of prisoners before me…?" I pause when a thought strikes me. "So if none of the others have left…why me?" I'm still suspicious; my eyes scan the room watching the others, a voice in my brain yells at me to flee back into the night.

Marcus bends close to Annaliese's ear and whispers. In a louder voice, he prods her on. "Go ahead…tell him."

She stares at the ground and nervously shuffles her feet. The murmuring in the room stops. I look around at the others. Again, nobody meets my gaze.

Annaliese shuffles a while longer, then starts quietly talking. I tilt my head close to hear her voice. "Several years back, a band of men were captured by our soldiers. The men were said to be plotting an attack and were apprehended before they could converge on the city."

Annaliese fell quiet. "Where they came from nobody knew...how they found our city was a mystery. The men wore clothing similar to yours."

"You have to understand," Annaliese lifted her eyes to meet mine, "The Prophets control every aspect of Adams City from what time we rise, to the food we eat and the way our days are spent. So if the Prophets proclaim the men dangerous, then we also believe that they are enemies."

"I was the only one aside from the guards, and the Prophets, allowed contact with the men. My father is the High Prophet." Annaliese pauses. She turns her head in Marcus's direction for assurance before continuing. "I delivered food to the prisoners while they were detained in the cages. During their stay, I talked with them, curious to know where they came from, why they would spy on us, why they wanted to do us harm." Annaliese's voice grows quiet. I wait patiently, wondering what this has to do with me.

"The stories the men told varied greatly from the reports released by the Prophets. We were told the men had been captured while conspiring to attack the city. At first, I disregarded the prisoner's pleas of innocence. Why wouldn't they lie to me, I reasoned, the men would say anything to gain their freedom? You see, very few of us have ever wandered outside the city limits, other than short walks into the lava fields. But no one dares venture to the surface. In fact, very few of us would even know how to get there."

"The Prophet's words are and always have been law in this city, so we had no reason to question the charges against the prisoners. After spending time with them, I began having doubts that these men sought to harm us. The prisoners told me they were on the surface, transporting supplies in their ice sled, when our soldiers ambushed them."

The term ice sled snags my attention. "What did these men look like? How long ago was this?" I blurt out the questions. Numerous teams from the New Capital had been lost over the years while running the surface, could this really be one of our crews?

Annaliese looks away, her eyes glancing down at the floor, her voice barely a whisper. "One of the men said he was an explorer. He told me that he was the pilot of the vessel and his crew was returning home with a cargo of metals and fuels. He pleaded with the Prophets to let them go, that his city was in dire need of these supplies." She continues ignoring my queries, her voice low, almost inaudible. "This man was much older…but he looked a lot like you, Mike." Finishing, she raises her head to look at me, the rims of her eyes wet, a tear slowly meandering down her cheek.

I am speechless. Through narrowed eyelids, I regard the girl standing in front of me, memories of my father's last voyage replaying in my mind. I was a teenager when my father and his crew failed to return to the Capital. More victims of the frozen, unforgiving surface of this desolate planet. The loss of my father was the reason I became an ice racer.

I travelled the surface, secretly hoping that one day I would stumble across my father's lost ship and at least have a chance to bid my final farewell. Over the years, my hopes waned. As time dragged on, reality set in and his memory started to fade. I came to accept the fact that he was gone, and I would never see him again…and now this.

Could what she say be true? Was it even possible that after so many years, my father could still be alive? Or was this some kind of cruel joke?

Annaliese had to be mistaken. My father and his crew perished on the surface, like many others before and after, unable to survive the blizzards and winds and freezing temperatures that ruled the topside of the planet. And now, she tells me they may be here? I face her, speechless, my thoughts wavering between hope and disbelief.

Finally, I find my voice. "So he is here now, in the oil mines you talk about, or held as a prisoner elsewhere in your city? Can you take me to him?

More tears ring Annaliese's eyes and streak down her face. She looks me in the eye, her head shaking.

" I am so sorry," she cries.

Chapter 13

My Father

The room is silent. My eyes mist while a flood of emotions pour over me. At first, the thought of my father held prisoner in this city saddens me, and then anger replaces my sorrow. I look at the walls searching for answers.

"How…when did he…" I can't bring myself to finish the sentence. I am overwrought with emotions…despair, sorrow and anger. I glance around the room, starting and stopping to speak, my mind spinning.

A hand reaches out and takes mine. Annaliese watches my face, tears staining hers. Breathing deeply, I fight to control my feelings.

"What happened?" I ask in a much calmer tone than I feel. "Did you talk to him much, how did he…die?"

I ask her to tell me everything about his internment here. She leads me over to a cluster of chairs. When we sit, she composes herself and, choking back tears she starts at the beginning. The day the crew from my father's sled was escorted into the city.

"Word about the capture of our enemies rippled through the city before they arrived." Annaliese recalled. "The soldiers marched the prisoners, each man gagged and bound hand and foot in chains, from the far end of the city, an area close to the mine entrance. The Prophets encouraged us to show our gratitude for the returning troops and a large crowd awaited their return."

Annaliese and I sat to the side of the room chatting, for hours. I felt anger well inside when she told me of the treatment my father and his men experienced as they were marched through the crowd toward the cages. The Prophets, Annaliese said, stirred the crowd with stories of horror and rants about the atrocities that would have befallen Adams Mountain if these men were successful in their attack. The crowd became agitated by the prophets' words, angry and abusive toward the prisoners.

"I have to confess that I felt this way, too. We are a peaceful community, so why would these men descend on us with ill intentions." Annaliese admitted. "The prophets' words painted the men as incarnates of the devil, with the most evil intentions."

The captives were locked in cages for close to a week while they waited the prophets' judgement. Annaliese's face brightens as she tells me of the conversations she had with my father.

At first, she admits, she was scared and intimidated by the strange men. After the prophets' harsh claims, she was uncertain and she ignored the repeated attempts at conversation by the men, but slowly she overcame her fear and grew curious about the lives and the world these men called home.

The prisoners spent hours regaling her with stories about their life, of the ice dome they called a city, the harsh struggle to survive and the brutal journeys they faced on the surface. A surface that was as alien to her as this shiny city was to them.

She stops her story and smiles, more to herself than to me. "Your father was very proud of you. He bragged about you, you know. His only regret, he told me, was that he would not have a chance to see you one more time." The smile, like the thought, fades.

"When I saw you locked in that cage a few days ago, I was certain you were his son. I didn't know what I should do, but in my heart I knew that I couldn't let you end up like the others."

She looks at me, tears welling in her eyes. A trace of a smile returns to her face. I'm stumped. I don't know what to do or say. I choke out a thanks and wait for her to continue.

She told me of the mock trial the prisoners faced and how, in the end, they were branded dangerous enemies of the city and sentenced to work in the oil mines. Having no idea what oil mines are, I ask her to explain?

"The mines," she says, "are a group of open pits and caves, oil saturates the soil. The mines have been worked since the founding of Adams Mountain. The mines are a blessing and are the source of fuel that powers the city. The mines, I believe, are the reason the prophets chose this site, to begin with, and ever since they have fought to keep the location secret from outsiders." She pauses, relating the city's history.

"Centuries ago, when the earth shook and the skies clouded with volcano dust, the prophets were blamed for the approaching apocalypse." A flash of anger passes quickly across her face at the unpleasant memory of the treatment of her ancestors, "supposedly because of a war they unleashed on the world. Our people were hunted mercilessly, the original founders only way to escape annihilation at the hands of our enemies was by retreating to Adams Mountain. This city became a refuge. Then, according to our history, the climate on the surface collapsed when the volcanoes rained destruction over the globe. When the dust and ash filled the atmosphere and blocked the sun and the snow and cold arrived, our ancestors were trapped here."

"As the temperature continued cooling and the surface slowly became uninhabitable, the prophets and their followers tore apart the giant metal wind machines and used the materials to construct the city. This is our history, but I believe that Adams Mountain existed before this happened. Certain materials that still are in use to this day like the wood used for doors and forms of technology that don't figure into the timeline. I think that the original prophet, Lucas, had the foresight to begin construction of Adams Mountain before the climate turned on mankind." The story continued.

"Much of our history details his exploits. From his attempts as a young man to save the environment, the women who stood by his side, to his massive following, right up to the time of his death. A sad account of how after all of his sacrifices, the way he was treated at the end, governments hunting him, the world blaming his climate war for destroying the environment, a situation that surely he couldn't control, and at the end, his broken heart while witnessing his precious world self destruct." Annaliese grew red in the face, the stories of her youth conjuring an ingrained defensiveness to her words. I watch her wrestle with the conflicting theories both for and against the city's founder and his methods."

"Lucas died of a heart attack shortly after taking refuge in this city." She sat silent lost in her thoughts.

"Regardless," she continues. "By some miracle, the heat from the buildings and the proximity to the mountain's volcano kept the snow and ice from smothering the city. As the snow covered the surrounding area and the cold increased, the combination of heated air shielded the city and over the decades formed an ice dome to shroud and protect us."

"The oil mines. Who works them, where are they?" Then the question I am skirting around. I hesitate before asking. "Can I go there? Is that where my father is buried, are there any others from his crew..." a lump collects in my throat as I force the words out. "...Is there some reminder of him there?"

She shakes her head but won't meet my eyes. "I'm so sorry," she says again as if she was personally to blame for his death. The talking in the room is still hushed, leaving me to deal with the news. I sit inert. I had never grieved for the loss of my father before, because I held out a flicker of hope that one day I would meet him again.

For hours, I remain lost in my thoughts, memories of my father and the brief time we shared together playing over again in my mind.

A rustling by some of the others pulls me out of my reverie. I watch while several of Annaliese's group don the military robes they had worn when I arrived, many appear to be ready to leave.

Leaving the chairs, I walk over to where the people are gathered. I stand outside of the group, listening to them talk. The discussion ends and some leave the room. When only Annaliese and a couple of others remain, I turn to her. She notices the puzzled look on my face.

"The city will be awakening soon. The others have to return to their homes before their absence is noticed," she explains.

"What about you," I ask but as the words leave my mouth the sacrifice she has made for my freedom strikes home. "Won't your father and the others wonder how I escaped?" I wait for her to answer, but the question is rhetorical.

She looks at me then turns away. Quietly she murmurs. "They will know."

"You were the only one who had access?" I hope I am wrong in my assumption, but I don't think so.

She walks away and leaves me standing alone. Marcus leaves his position by the door and comes to my side.

"She can't return home, can she?" I see the sadness in his eyes.

"No. Like you, the prophets will hunt Annaliese," he replies solemnly. "She knew the risk she was taking when we helped you escape," he adds. "We tried to talk her out of doing it, but she said she was willing to make that choice."

"What will happen now?"

"Well...I suppose we hide down here while the Prophet's men tire of searching the city and convince themselves the two of you have left."

"Will they?" My tone is underlined with worry, not so much for myself but for Annaliese, the daughter of the High Prophet.

"I'm not sure. Nobody has ever escaped the city before."

"Is there a way out, a way back to the surface?"

"There must be, but I know of none who have tried." He ponders my inquiry. "The prophets regularly send men to the surface on excursions, but how and why is not something that they share."

"So what now?" she asks.

"We hide here and hope that they don't discover us." I fire back. "How many people know about this room and the tunnels under the city that lead to here?"

"Very few." He answers. "This small group you met here is all. We discovered these tunnels years ago and had kept them secret."

"How long do you think they will search?"

"Again. I can't say. The prophets are unbending with their rules, their authority demands they act without any leniency."

I leave Marcus and wander over to where Annaliese stands.

"I guess I'm the one who should be sorry." I apologize. She turns to me and puts on a brave face.

All through the day and into the next evening, we wait and bide our time. It is nerve-wracking staying hidden and not knowing what is taking place on the streets above. In the back of my mind, I expect the Prophet's guards to come bursting through the door at any moment.

Idly chatting, Marcus and Annaliese tell me about the demanding and dangerous labour that awaits those who the prophets sentence to the mines.

"There can't possibly be enough..." I searched for the right word. Prisoners were the only word I could think of to describe foreigners to this hidden city. "Prisoners to work the mines and I can't see the people of Adams Mountain wanting to volunteer for the job. Not if it is as dangerous as you describe?" I wait for an answer, trying to picture in my mind how this city functions.

Marcus explains how people who question the prophets or challenge city laws are subjected to work in the mines. An effective way to discourage dissidence and to quell resistance to the leaders he assured me.

"And apparently there is no shortage of malcontents to fill the labour rolls," he adds. "Every one of us knows people charged with crimes against the city. Friends and relatives who've disappeared into the black pit for trumped-up reasons."

I leave Marcus' company, needing time to myself. I move off alone and dig out my reading paper as a distraction. I try to ease my mind from the waiting and worrying over our dire situation.

Annaliese joins me later. "I have seen old papers like yours before," she says.

"I thought your history records began when this city came into existence?" I ask.

"All the public ones do, yes." She clarifies. "But years ago when we discovered these tunnels Marcus stumbled across old records hidden in a cave under the city. The writings in those papers are very similar to your reading page."

"You didn't turn them over to your father?" I ask.

"No. When Marcus showed me the papers we agreed to keep them hidden. Over the years, we have heard rumblings, rumours really, that the history taught us by the prophets, my father included, was written to support their teachings, a way to keep the people of the city from questioning the Prophet's authority. So at the time, we presumed they were the writings of some disgruntled faction, but now…"

Throughout the day, members of Marcus' group stop by the hidden room to keep us updated on the search rolling across the city. The city is on lockdown as the Prophet's men comb the streets checking each building, pursuing me for capture.

The leaders of Adams Mountain are prohibiting residents from leaving their homes. The news came to us that the city was at a standstill, the lives of the prophets' followers halted because of the lockdown. The already nervous population locked themselves indoors afraid of what might happen.

Marcus says he has never seen a search of this magnitude before. Crime in Adams Mountain was minimal, and the residents are too afraid of the prophets, so there will be no place for us to hide.

The city has a small underground resistance of sorts to the ruling prophets, but it has never grown big enough to cause the leaders of the city any worry. Aside from watching a few of the resistance from a distance, the leaders tolerate the small, secretive gatherings. Some members of the underground's names are known by the Military Guards. Individuals and groups are spied upon but never to the extent where a general population was harassed or even locked down.

Annaliese and I are talking on the far side of the room when the door is flung open, interrupting us. One of the men who were here when I first arrived rushes in and pulls Marcus aside. Annaliese and I jump up and hurry over.

"Daniel was taken by the guards to meet the prophets," the man tells Marcus. "Daniel wasn't going voluntarily, by the way he was struggling." The young man pauses, his demeanour telegraphs trouble. "Daniel knows the location of this room and that these two hide here," He states, "what if he talks?"

Chapter 14

The Tunnels

Marcus wheels around and looks at us, "He's right. It won't be safe here for the two of you much longer." Turning his attention back to the young man, Marcus sends him away with new instructions.

"Go back into the tunnels and keep an eye on the entrance. We'll need a few minutes to prepare. Warn us if the guards get close." The man nods and scoops a robe from the pile on the floor before he disappears back down the tunnel.

"What are you thinking?" Annaliese asks Marcus.

"Grab some supplies." Marcus lifts one of the discarded robes and throws it over his shoulders. "We'll go deeper in the tunnels...from there, I don't know, but we'll figure it out when we get there."

I watch Annaliese rush to a pile of sacks stacked against a wall and rummage through them, assembling a collection of food and water. She places the items into a smaller bag. When she finishes, she returns to our side.

"Where do these tunnels run? Are they under the whole city?" I ask.

Marcus shakes his head. "No. They'll keep us out of sight for a while, but we will eventually come to a dead end. There we'll have to ascend to the streets."

I grab the sack of supplies from Annaliese. Marcus passes me a flashlight, takes a last look around the room and then cautiously steps into the hall before signalling us to join him.

Marcus leads us a short distance down the tunnel before ducking into an intersecting tunnel that alters the direction of our escape. The path leads away from the original entrance. The lava shafts morph from a comfortable open space to a much tighter space where we have to squeeze and crawl through short sections.

The three of us scramble through the labyrinth of rock tunnels in silence. How Marcus knows where each tunnel leads and what direction to follow is beyond me. We follow after him from tunnel to tunnel. Walking in some, crawling through others.

The smell of sulphur from the volcanic rock hangs in the stale air. The confined spaces grow humid and tight, but still Marcus leads on at as fast as we can manage.

Coming to a halt in a closet-sized cavern, Marcus begins to speak.

"We are going to have to surface not far from here. These tunnels stop beneath a street a few blocks from the entrance to the oil mine," he says, his attention focused on Annaliese

"Is that where you are leading us?" Annaliese asks, with an evident note of surprise.

"There's nowhere else to go." He diverts his eyes. "You know that your dad will have the city torn apart searching for the two of you. The people in this town are afraid of your father, and most will never consider helping or hiding you for fear of retribution. Even for a short time," he adds.

On our journey, Marcus gives me a brief breakdown of the small band of resistance that has been growing in the city opposed to the iron-fisted rule of the prophets. He says the population's objections to the strict-living conditions has been festering for years, but the majority are too scared to challenge them for fear of being exiled to the oil mines or even worse.

"The people," he says, "hard working, decent men and women, who have grown weary of the dictatorship and guardedly voice their displeasure when among their closest friends. At the same time they regard their neighbours suspiciously wondering if they are spies for the prophets. This sense of distrust through the community helps the prophets maintain their power."

"Well, why can't we leave the same way I arrived?" I ask, realizing we are on our own with nowhere to hide and no one else to count on.

"No. The path ends not far from the city. A giant crevice in the rock formation makes it impossible to cross. There have been stories of people who have died trying to traverse it." Marcus replies.

"Then how about along the lava river, surely we could follow it away from here."

"The canyon narrows making that route impassable too. Besides, the heat from the melted rock would kill you before you travel very deep into it." Marcus releases a quick breath, his mind foraging for an answer. "Your only hope will be to gain access and then cross the pit and try for the air chute. I have heard it leads to the surface."

I look at Marcus, confused by his words.

"The surface," I repeat. "Annaliese doesn't have a thermal suit. How would she survive? I don't know this place at all, but I have to believe there is another choice. She would not survive on the surface, not even for a short period," I protest. In my mind, I search for a more suitable solution. "Hell, I don't even know if I could survive on the surface without a sled full of luck."

Annaliese gently touches my arm.

"They will kill you if they catch you," she states matter-of-factly. "We don't have much of a choice."

"What will happen if they catch you?" I search her face.

She turns to look at Marcus; the two exchange a knowing look.

"I'll be alright," she mumbles, but her face pales in the glow of the flashlight.

"How about you, Marcus? If your friend talks, will the guards not know that you, too, helped me?" There is obviously something they aren't telling me. I push further. "I am not going another step until you guys level with me."

"Dissidents get sent to the oil mine as punishment," he quietly confirms. "I can deal with the consequences. Annaliese should be okay. Her father is the High Prophet." He doesn't sound convinced.

"So the only real option we have is if the three of us leave the city? That is the only choice I will accept. If the three of us can't escape, then you two should turn me in and tell Annaliese's father that you recaptured me. I won't let you take the fall for me. You don't even know me. The two of you suffering because of me is insane!"

"Let's cross the city and find a way into the mines. Once there we can worry about what to do after," Marcus declares. "We still need to get out of these tunnels. Once the guards start searching down here, we will be trapped, and we won't have any choices."

We move on, Marcus in the lead, as we snake through more tunnels. Suddenly, the beam from Marcus' flashlight shines on a wall of solid lava with notches chiselled into the wall every few inches.

"Turn the lights off," Marcus whispers and jams his foot into a notch. He holds the flashlight with his mouth and his hands reach for support as he begins to climb. In the blackness, Annaliese and I wait. The only sound in the darkness comes from Marcus' feet rubbing against the rock; he climbs slowly working higher. The scraping of his feet on the rock is joined at intervals by the sound our nervous breathing.

A high-pitched grinding of metal signals his arrival at the top of the climb. Then a light flashes back down, lighting the wall and the floor.

"It's clear. Hurry, climb," he urges. The beam of his flashlight shines down the jagged wall for us. I motion for Annaliese to go ahead of me, and then with a quick look back down the tunnel, I brace my foot on the wall and follow her to the street above.

Marcus grabs Annaliese's hand, lifting her onto the street. I climb from the hole, close behind. On the street, we stand restlessly while Marcus quietly lowers the lid, hiding the tunnel's entrance before we creep to a side of the alley.

In the shadow of a building, we wait again while Marcus adjusts his military disguise. Finishing, he motions for us to follow, leading to the end of the alley. Marcus stops and points.

"We've got about another six blocks until we see the entrance to the mine," he says in a harsh whisper. "If we are lucky enough to cover the distance undetected, we still have to find our way past the guards at the entrance and then down into the pit before we can cross it."

He had already explained to me how the mines were closely guarded. Not defended from the people on the city streets, because no one would intentionally venture into the pit, but to ensure that the felons serving life at the bottom had no chance of escape. The Prophets are extremely protective of the mines, he tells me. Without them, the city would surely perish.

He signals us to move. We creep silently along in the shadows, our target the opening of another alley that will lead us on a direct route toward the mines.

Ten strides away from the opening we had just come through, a stern voice calls to us.

"Identify yourself." Guards materialize at the opposite end of the block, their guns raised as they step out of the shadows. The three of us stop dead in our tracks.

Chapter 15

Run for Freedom

"Follow my lead," Marcus whispers as he takes a quick step behind Annaliese and myself.

He alerts the guards. "Over here." Marcus waves, purposely calling attention to us. "I found these two sneaking around this alley." With a shove from behind, Marcus pushes us forward to meet the military guards.

The guards watch our approach. The men slowly lower their raised guns. My heart beats rapidly in my chest at the thought of being returned to the cage. Annaliese nervously looks between Marcus, the guards and then up at me as, step-by-step, we walk closer to capture. I find myself wondering how much I trust Marcus. We've only met a day earlier and for all I know, he might be looking to escape prosecution by turning us in.

"Stop," Marcus commands as we come within feet of the guards. Stepping to the front of us, Marcus stands to the side of the men drawing their attention.

I have no idea what he is thinking, but seeing the opportunity, I rush the guard on the right. My hand clasps his gun arm, my shoulder ramming into the guy's chest, driving him back into a wall.

We struggle. The man is strong, but I can feel my adrenaline spike from fear and the thought of recapture. A blow to my injured arm send jolts of pain running to my brain, my eyes tear. Anger rises with the pain. Raising my right hand, I drive a fist into the man's stomach, leaving the guard winded.

He doubles over, catching my rising knee in his face. The sickening crunch of breaking facial bones follows. The guard's gun falls from his grip and he falls to the street. I bend to retrieve the weapon and whirl around in time to see the butt of Marcus' rifle connect with the other guard's face.

The two of us stand looking down at the fallen men. Marcus takes their weapons and passes them along with his own to Annaliese.

"Help me peel their uniforms off," he says to me in between rasping breaths of air. He leans down to pull the robe off one of the dazed guards.

Standing, he throws the robe at me. "Wear this," he says, and waits while I change.

The two of us drag the unconscious men into the deep shadows of the buildings. Marcus rummages under his robe and produces a knife. Slashing and cutting at my discarded brown robe, he cuts strips of cloth and passes them to me.

"Bind their hands and feet and gag them." He calls out, his hands busy cutting pieces from the robe. We work fast. The fear of being discovered by other guards patrolling the streets is heavy on our mind.

With the stolen guns in hand and wearing the military robes as disguise we leave the area at a brisk walk, blending into the cover of the buildings. Marcus takes the lead, walking a few steps in front of us to scout for any other unwanted company.

"A few more blocks," Marcus says pointing ahead. His breathing is still laboured from the brush with the prophets' men and the tension we are all feeling. We move as quickly as we dare, while maintaining all the caution we can afford.

At an intersection on the road, he raises his hand signalling a stop. Annaliese and I wait and watch while Marcus slips to the edge of the alley and peers into the front street. What he is watching, we have no idea, but he remains silent and unmoving. Something around the corner is obviously troubling him.

After several minutes he returns, his face a clear map of what lies in the path of our escape. Marcus shakes his head and in a hushed voice he tells us what we face.

"The door to the mines is across the street," he says. He is clearly distracted. "The problem facing us is a sizable group of the soldiers gathered around the entrance." I find that I am holding my breath as I wait for him to reveal what else is troubling him.

"The only way through will be to draw them away from the entrance."

"There's not another way to the mines?" I ask. I realize that surprising the first two guards was more luck then we deserved, but to my thinking, trying the same trick against a larger group would require more luck than the three of us had. I search Marcus' face, and I know he is has the same thoughts.

He shakes off my question. "The wall separating the mines from the city is solid steel and embedded into the rock cliffs. The door is our only access."

"What can we do to distract them? There has to be some trick, otherwise we will have to split up?" I think quickly, not willing to accept that solution. "We can try and shoot our way past them, but that would no doubt draw every guard in the city down to this area," I think aloud.

"No. Shooting has to be our last resort. Give me a minute, I'll figure out something. There has to be a way."

The three of us huddle in the shadows. Together, we search for a way past the men blocking our only chance of escape. Suddenly, Marcus jumps to his feet, an idea forming in his mind. "On my signal, you two run for the door."

"What are you going to do?" Annaliese asks, her voice laden with worry.

"I'll create a distraction, draw as many guards away from the door as I can," he replies, his feet already moving before we can protest. He creeps back to the edge of the building where the streets meet, pauses a second and then disappears from our sight.

I grab Annaliese's hand and we rush to the end of the building. Confused, we peer around the corner and down the street in the direction Marcus entered. Clinging tight to the walls of the building, we watch as he scuttles down the side, walking ever closer to the gate. Two-thirds of the way, he crosses the street toward a gap opposite us.

I feel Annaliese's breath on my neck. The two of us remain hidden behind the corner, wondering what Marcus has planned. He suddenly leaves the safety of his hiding spot and jumps into the street, waving his hands and hollering toward the guarded gate.

"Here," he cries and waves his arms frantically until he has the guard's attention. "Over here. Hurry, over here. I just saw the prisoner at the end of alley. Quickly, he's turning the corner." Marcus points down into the alley, waving his arms urging the guards to hurry. When the men leave their post, Marcus runs into the opening and disappears.

Annaliese stares wide-eyed as she witnesses Marcus' ploy. I keep my eyes on the door. A solitary guard is left to protect the entrance; the others rush down the street chasing after Marcus. Straightening quickly, I turn to Annaliese whispering instructions.

"Stay tight to the building. We will only have one chance to creep close to the guard while his attention is on the alley." I slip around the corner pulling, Annaliese along and then move fast using the building for cover. The distance from the corner to the door is not far.

The whole time we are on the move, I keep my eyes locked on the guard's face, expecting him to hear our footsteps and turn in our direction. His gaze remains on the alley where the others ran. Running in front of Annaliese, the guard and the door draw closer. Twenty feet away, the guard is turned in the other direction. Fifteen feet. Ten feet.

With a yard left separating us, the guard spins and looks right at us. Confused at the sight of us racing toward him, he is slow to react. Leaving Annaliese, I quicken my stride. My momentum carries me into the surprised man.

Using the advantage of surprise and the guard's own confusion, I lower my head and charge forward, my shoulder contacting his chest. The rifle flies out of my hands as the force of the collision carries us both backward until we hit the wall at an angle. I hear the man's breath rush out of his mouth as he becomes pinned between the weight of my body and the rigid wall.

I trip and fall away from the guard. He regains his footing first, swings his weapon and stands over me. Before he can raise his gun, the man stops, staggers and then falls in my direction.

Annaliese is standing with her hands still in the air. She's facing me. Her stolen rifle clutched in her hands like a club. I nod my thanks and scramble to my feet, dusting off my robe before I bend and retrieve my fallen gun.

I rush to the door and try the handle, only to find it locked. The door doesn't budge. Stepping back to the fallen guard, I empty his pockets. Precious seconds wasted, and I fail to find a key of any type. I roll the man onto his back. A chain slips from beneath his collar as I move him. I grasp the chain and pull. A key slides into view. Quickly I yank my fist back snapping the chain.

I raise my hand in triumph and show the key to Annaliese then return to the door. The key slips easily into the hole, the lock turns smoothly. The clunking of the bolt releasing is loud. Twisting the handle, I slowly nudge the door inward, prepared to encounter more armed guards waiting on the other side. The area is deserted. A vast cavern bathed by bright light greets my eyes.

Passing Annaliese my rifle, I rush over to the prone guard, motioning for Annaliese to go through the door. I lift the guard by his arms and drag him with me. Safely on the other side, I relock the door before taking a moment to study the lit expanse and reassure myself that our actions are unobserved.

Stripping the guard of his robe, I tear the cloth and tie the man's arms and legs, then stuff a gag in his mouth, following the same procedure Marcus used earlier with the men in the alley. When I finish, I roll the unconscious guard tight against the bottom of the door before reclaiming my gun from Annaliese. Holding the rifle by its barrel, I raise it shoulder height then drive the butt hard into the guard's head. I stop to take a breath and then straighten checking on Annaliese. The two of us turn and survey the enormous cavern containing the oil mines.

We stand together in silence. We are stunned at the sight surrounding us. Not many feet away to the left of the door, a solid wall of rock rises. The rock wall runs all the way to the underside of the cavern's ceiling. Opposite the door, about 20 feet from where we stand is a metal railing. On the far side of the rail, a stone shelf drops storeys below us.

I trace the rail with my eyes. It runs to our right, several hundred feet farther along the shelf, ending at a structure that sits extended over the edge of the drop-off. Large steel brackets angle from the underside of the building back toward a rock face.

I look over at the building before walking away from the door toward the metal railing. The crater beyond the protective rail is massive. The far side of the pit is barely visible, even with the bright lights that illuminate the cavern.

Annaliese follows me to the rail. Certain that our entrance went undetected, I look down, my hands tightly gripping the round metal rail cap. I can't help but gawk dumbstruck at the open pit far below us.

Chapter 16

The Cliff Building

Thoughts of escape are momentarily forgotten. Speechless, we grip the iron rail, transfixed by the sight of the large bowl carved out below us. The layers of rock have been removed, exposing deeper rings of bedrock. Machinery and men on the floor below claw and scrape away the ground in an unending search for oil deposits.

Like giant dinosaurs, metal structures rise and lower, their large steel wheels rotating in a macabre symphony of scraping, straining steel, their grinding and squealing adding to the rhythm of the surreal scene.

The workers look tiny from our vantage point high above them. They walk among the machinery, their collective voices drifting up to join the loudness of earth-drilling equipment. Accompanying the sounds of men and machines is the overpowering stench of exposed oil deposits and damp rotting earth.

The noxious fumes of the nearby molten lava mixed with the sweltering heat and volcanic ash assault our noses. If there actually is a hell, like the one the elders speak of waiting in the afterlife, I am positive that it would resemble the Adams Mountain oil pit.

My coughing in the thick, choking atmosphere breaks my trance. Out of the corner of my eye, I see Annaliese. She's holding the folds of her robe tight to her face to block the intrusion of foul air. I pull my helmet from under my robe and against her protests, brush back her hood and slip the visor over her head, tighten it around her neck, then adjust the air scrubber.

Annaliese becomes still. The expression on her face changes, the pupils of her eyes growing larger and her face pales. At first, I think there is a problem with my helmet but she raises a finger and points behind me. Glancing over my shoulder, I follow the direction of her finger. Guards are walking toward us from the cliff building.

"How good are you with that gun?" I whisper. She shrugs her shoulders. "When I give you a signal, lift the gun and shoot." I spin on my heels and walk to meet the men from the cliff building. I use my body to shield Annaliese's movements from the sight of the approaching guards.

I raise my hand in a friendly gesture, and when I am only several yards away, I signal for

Annaliese to fire while I drop to the ground. Bullets whistle over my head. The men from the cliff building are slow to respond. One twists as a bullet bites into his side, the other dives to the side, his rifle clatters loosely on the rock shelf. The diving man comes to rest against the metal railing that protects the edge of the cliff.

I swing my gun up and squeeze the trigger. My aim is not accurate, but with the two of us shooting, the guards are trapped and unprepared.

Not far behind us, the sounds of banging from the locked door at the mine entrance join the myriad of noise emanating from the pit. Risking a glance, I see the door shaking in time to the pounding. The guard I had bound and jammed against the bottom of the door, preventing it from opening.

"We have to move," I yell back at Annaliese and jump up from the ground and sprint ahead, my rifle covering the stunned guards. Without waiting for Annaliese, I move toward the guards with quick, long strides. The guard Annaliese shot is lying on the ground, clutching his wound. His buddy lays pinned against the rail, cowering, watching the barrel of my rifle.

Closing in I kick the fallen guns aside and stand over the guards. Annaliese joins me.

"Grab their rifles," I urge. With the barrel of my rifle, I motion the men to their feet, pointing at the cliff building "Move." I bark at them. I dare not risk another look back at the door to the mine, but the hair on my neck bristles. With our backs to the entrance door, I prepare myself for shouts ordering us to stop and a bullet in the back.

Moving with urgency, I shove the guards to speed things up. Following close behind the men, we enter the building. Inside the door, I close and lock it before I search the small space. We are standing in the crowded interior of a single-roomed shack. The walls are carved from rock and reinforced with steel; a wall contains a window overlooking the mine entrance.

Counters are fastened to one of the walls and a table with several chairs line another exterior wall. The far wall in the room, adjacent from where we had entered the building, hosts a pair of steel doors that overlap in the middle. On a raised counter to the right of the doors there is a panel with buttons protruding from its surface.

Pushing the guards toward the chairs, I turn to Annaliese, a puzzled expression on my face.

"Is there no way down into the mine from here?" I ask, unable to hide my disappointment at the fact that this building has no stairs leading into the pit. What is this room, what use is it? How are the prisoners transported into the mine? Annaliese nods her head at the panel with the buttons beside the overlapping doors.

"There is an elevator behind those doors," she explains. "It lowers on pulleys." She tells me. "What the hell is an elevator?" I want to ask but leave the question for later. There is enough on our mind at the moment.

She whirls on the unwounded guard, the barrel of her gun aimed at his head. "Show me how it works." She points to the panel. The guard glowers, refusing to answer. I raise my rifle and jam it into the chest of the wounded man.

"Now!" I threaten. "Or we will find out how the elevator works once you two are dead." Nervously, the guard walks past Annaliese, his eyes straying to the barrel of my rifle as he moves to the panel. Standing beside the box of buttons, he explains how the elevator functions. Once Annaliese is satisfied she will be able to operate the elevator, she motions with her head for the guard to take his seat beside his partner.

"Are you certain you can work that?" I get the same shrug she gave me when I asked her about the rifle.

"Sit down," I yell at the guard and follow him to the chairs. I stare the man in the eye. I ponder how best to subdue two men. The wounded guard moans, his face pale from pain, his hand pressed tight to the wound in his side, blood soaking his uniform.

The second guard looks between the wounded man and me and then back to his partner. My rifle butt catches the man in the side of the head as he's looking away. The guard crumples in his chair.

To the wounded man, I mumble, "Sorry." My rifle smashes into his head.

I grab a chair from the table and jam it under the door lever, then look out the window back down the ledge toward the mine entrance. I can see men starting to push it open.

"We've got to go." I step over and stand in front of the overlapping doors, waiting for Annaliese to show me this elevator. I watch as she presses the buttons. A whirring sound radiates from behind the doors, and with a grind they slide apart, revealing a small metal room.

"Move to the back," Annaliese tells me then hits another button and rushes in to join me. I stand with my back tight against the wall, Annaliese in front of me. The doors slide closed, and we wait.

The metal room shakes and with a jolt and clang it starts to lower. Slow at first and then gaining speed. Not really fast, but hopefully fast enough for us to escape before the prophets' men break into the cliff building.

Chapter 17

Into the Depths of Hell

My nerves match the shaking and wobbling of the descending room. Annaliese reaches for my hand and calms me by explaining the workings of this closed room that lowers on chains. The clanking and grinding of the pulleys and the motor accompany us as we crawl deeper into the mines

Fighting off the uneasiness I feel, I think ahead to when the doors open by telling Annaliese to crouch tight to the side with her gun ready. I do the same. Neither of us knows what to expect when the room reaches the bottom. Certainly, there must be guards on the floor of the mine, and I expect the guards to be waiting when the doors slide open.

The chamber continues downward. I glance at Annaliese, her eyes wide behind the plate of my visor. A trickle of sweat snakes down my back, the hairs on my neck tingle with uncertainty.

With a clunk and jerk, the room wobbles and then settles. Again, I glance in Annaliese's direction; her eyes are trained on the door, her gun held high and ready. I steady my sight on the doors and take a breath, waiting for them to open.

The doors shift and then grind open. The smells and noise pour into the small room before the doors yawn open, revealing the view at the bottom. Bright lights welcome our arrival into the pit. Guards stand clustered in the vicinity, a few men stand facing the opening, others have their backs to us as they patrol the area

There are too many men to take by surprise, so I tighten my finger around the trigger of the rifle. Simultaneously, I hear the bark of Annaliese's gun. Our bullets mow down the men closest to the open doors; the guards facing away from the elevator are caught by surprise. Our continuous stream of gunfire ends their threat. Leaving the metal box, I run, bent low, checking the guards. Crouched among the fallen men, I scan the area around the elevator for more of the prophets' guards.

A bullet crashes past my foot. The shot comes from somewhere high above. Diving to the side, I roll over to a stack of oil drums and search the cliff. I begin by checking the rock walls, then my eyes travel up to the rail on the rock ledge. Finally, I look all the way up to the opening at the cliff building. Men are leaning over the edge of the floor. The rifles in their hands pointed down, flashes of exploding gunpowder mark the end of the gun barrels as bullets smack the ground near me.

I panic. Where is Annaliese? In the brief exchange with the guards, I had forgotten about her. I look back at the metal room. She sits tight to the wall, hiding just inside the doors.

"I'll try to scare them. When I yell, you hurry over here," I call to her. Before she can answer, the barrel of my rifle lifts, the gun bucks in my hands with each shot fired. The gun is pointing almost straight up at the men hanging out of the building. My bullets are off target, but close enough to make the men duck back into the building for cover.

"Now!" I holler. Annaliese bolts from the elevator, her head lowered as she runs to join me.

"Wait here," I say and foolishly rush back to the fallen bodies by the elevator. Moving from guard to guard, I collect their rifles, my body tensed for the strike of bullets from the shooters above.

Carrying the firearms by their straps, I dash back behind the cover of the drums. I pass Annaliese a few of the rifles, then turn to leave. I lead us away from the metal room and wind my way around scattered crates, empty drums and rusted machinery, my eyes scanning the tangle of equipment for more guards.

The damp black ground diffuses the light, the air rank with the pungent smells of oil residue and volcanic gasses. We dart around the towering, rusted machinery scattered across the floor of the mine. Out of the corner of my eye I see a movement. A shadow dashes out of sight like a specter in a nightmare.

Swivelling my head around, I catch glimpses of other ethereal forms slipping among the tangle of machinery and piles of rock and debris. The air thick with a combination of fumes burns my throat, my eyes water.

Glancing back at the cliff building, I watch the elevator rise from the floor and climb upward. From the safety of a pillar I nudge Annaliese and motion deeper into the mine.

The two of us move warily and distance ourselves from the bottom of the elevator shaft, picking a path around the machinery and rocks, my eyes roaming to spot trouble before it find us.

A few hundred feet from the elevator, we round a pile of oily waste. Breathing heavily through my mouth I suck in mouthfuls of the putrid air. Peering around the mound, I see no sign of the prophets' men yet.

The sounds of scuffling feet scrape across the rocks behind us. Tensing, my hand on the rifle trigger, I whirl around. Staring back at us are strange-looking men and women. Their grime coated faces passive, curious, the whites of their eyes tracking our movements. I presume these unfortunate souls have been lowered into this pit to serve out their time. Their robes are stained and tattered, their faces haggard from the conditions of life in the mines.

More footsteps close in on us. All around, small pockets of the ragged mineworkers materialize; none of the people I see are wearing the robes of the military guards. I turn, looking in all directions, my gun at the ready in case they rush.

We stand face to face with the dispelled faction of the shiny city. Each face that watches us is stained with dirt and grease. One of the men advances closer to where we wait, a large wrench clutched tight in his hand.

"You are brave and obviously new down here," he scowls at me. "You should have learned better than to leave your post and venture this far into the labyrinth. Your people may keep us from returning to the city, but the floor of the mine is ours." He mocks us and the other miners voice displeasure at our appearance. "Foolish for only two guards to wander this far away from the safety of your brethren."

"Guards." I fail to understand the man's words. Annaliese tugs at my sleeve. The military robes we confiscated to aid in our escape convince them we are a threat. I lay the rifles at my feet and slip out of the stolen uniform.

"We are not the prophets' men. We stole these outfits for camouflage to shield us from detection. We've been on the run since Annaliese freed me from the cages." I explain the misconception of our meeting.

"Annaliese," a second pit worker questions and then steps forward to pull the hood of her robe back to reveal her helmeted face. Annaliese raises her arms, lifting my helmet from her head, a mixture of fear and defiance radiate from her eyes.

"The High Prophets daughter!" yet another exclaims.

"What kind of ploy are those fool prophets up to now? Sending you two among us, to do what?" The miner with the wrench eyes us suspiciously. "Your father has the nerve to send you down here?"

"She is here to help me escape the prophets." I stand up to the miner. "I was brought to this city as a prisoner. Why, I don't know. My being here was an accident and yet the prophets brand me as a danger to their people. Annaliese has forfeited her freedom in freeing me from the cages. If caught she will suffer the same fate as you for her kindness." Annaliese stands quietly. Anger emboldens me. I know the guards can't be far behind.

"I will shoot my way through your ranks if that is your decision." My eyes dart to the pile of rifles at my feet. I am afraid the guards will arrive soon. We have to move. "The prophets' men will swarm this area shortly in search of us, and I will not let them recapture me nor will I allow Annaliese to be punished by the prophets." We arrive at an impasse. Murmurs of the miners' voices rumble around us.

Without another word, the wrench-wielding miner beckons us to follow. I look over at Annaliese. She shrugs and motions with her head as she steps after the man. I scoop up the rifles and look back at the others in the group before I move. Most of them have melted back into the surroundings.

With a quick pace, the miners move effortlessly through the mire of rock and metal leading us deeper into the labyrinth of the oil mine. The soles of our boots crunch as we pass over uneven ground and slurp through puddles of thick oil that fills the holes in the trail. As my foot finds such a hole, my feet slide on the oily ground, throwing me off balance. I twist and stumble. The guns I carry colliding with a metal frame and trip me, sending me to the ground.

One of the miners stops and helps me with a hand up. My thermal suit is now saturated with grime and oil residue. Reaching down to pick up the confiscated rifles, I pass them to the man who helped me. Passing the last gun, I straighten up.

The man I have passed the guns to stares from me to the guns and back again. I don't know what he is thinking, but I stand before him unarmed. He selects one of the rifles and passes it back to me; the other guns he redistributes to the small group accompanying us.

I nod my thanks, and he turns. We continue moving. The leader of the group stops at the end of the path and holds up his hand. The trail opens into a broad clearing. In the midst of the clearing stands a platform with a metal tower in the centre. Men and women are on the platform, bustling about among pipes and levers and cables.

"That's an oil derrick," the leader informs me, as if he can read my mind. I continue to stare at the metal tower as he leads on, his route turning and bringing us close to the piles of debris surrounding the opening. At the next break in the rubble, we leave the open floor and walk down a shrouded path leading toward the canyon wall.

A wall that appeared solid from a distance is broken up by shadowed holes. The lights of the oil mine fade as we draw closer to the wall. Annaliese and I follow the group into an opening in the wall and after several twists and turns, we arrive at the entrance to a cave.

"You can rest here for now." The leader tells us. Annaliese nudges me, my helmet held tight in her fingers.

"Do the guards not know about these caves?" I ask.

"They don't have to. Someone down here will eventually lead them to you." He says apologetically. "Our survival relies on the food and water the prophets allow the guards to bring for us daily. A threat to withhold our supplies will ease many tongues." The leader gives a brief lesson on how life in the oil mines work

"Every faction of life in the pit is controlled by the city. Water is pumped down from the surface, and food and other supplies even our clothing, the guards lower into the hole with the elevator."

"Any sign of an uprising is stemmed by the refusal of the life necessities. The food allotted is barely enough to survive on; our water comes rationed, as are other supplies. Our lives in these mines are hard, the conditions poor and the work is crippling. We have quotas to fill every day, and if we fail the punishment is to make us suffer more."

"Most of the people imprisoned here are barely hanging on, but they are not ready to admit defeat and die. So if it's between hiding you or extra rations for helping in your arrest, I am afraid they will reluctantly help the prophets recapture you. For that I am sorry."

"Is there no way out of here?" I ask, almost as a rhetorical question. These people would have had years to exploit any means of escape if there were one. The leader laughs.

"You two came down the only way back out of here." He kicks at some rocks on the cave floor. "And no. Even with these guns," he lifts the one he is carrying, "we can't force our way into the elevator."

"The controls are at the top of the cliff and even by capturing the guards at the bottom, the men at the top will never allow it. The guards deployed at the base know that their lives will be forfeit long before the elevator lowers under threat."

"I was told that there is a chute that pumps air from the surface. Is there no way to follow that to the surface?" I ask.

The leader gawks at me like I am a mere child. "I am sure a person could find a way up through it...you would freeze to death by the time you climbed a quarter of the way up." Then for the first time, he notices my heat suit under my robe. Furrowing his brow, the mineworker looks at Annaliese, then his focus swings back at me.

"You...you've been on the surface before, haven't you? So even if you could climb free, you probably couldn't survive up there for long." He pauses, struggling with his next statement. "I used to be one of the prophets' men selected for surface excursions. There is nothing around for miles and miles but snow and ice and blizzards." He turns his attention back to Annaliese.

"You are the daughter of the High Prophet, where would you go?" he asks in amazement. Before she can answer, we hear the sounds of loud voices echoing through the tunnels leading to the cave we are standing in.

"Do these caves lead anywhere?" I urgently ask.

"Eventually to the lava rivers, but the air and heat will kill you as fast as the cold on the surface will."

"We'll take our chances," I boldly reply.

"No," Annaliese protests. She pushes my visor toward me. "Both of us will not be able to escape, but with your suit and helmet you might have a chance."

"I won't leave without you," I tell her, stubbornly standing my ground. The voices in the tunnels grow louder as they move nearer the caves entrance, shadows fall across the opening of the cave. Annaliese steps closer to me and smiles.

"Good luck, Mike," She says. Before I know what's happening, she raises her hands, her palms forcefully driven into my chest. I stumble back, trip over a pile of rocks and fall into the mouth of a side tunnel, tumbling down a slight incline. Clambering to my feet, I hear the voices enter the big cave.

"Shit," I exclaim and pull back into the tunnel.

Chapter 18

The Heat of Hopelessness

With my back against a wall, standing in the darkest shadows of the tunnel, I listen. A loud exchange erupts from the cave. People scurry, the sound of running feet echoes louder, the activity followed by shouted commands, which I imagine, comes from the guards.

The excitement of voices rises in pitch, ringing off the cavern walls. Some are pleading, and others are in resignation. Then I hear a woman's voice, Annaliese, sounding anxious and defiant as she struggles. I put my hand on the rifle slung from my shoulder and clench my fist. I prepare to barge back into the cave and save her. Frozen with indecision, I listen to the angry shouting in the cave.

Imposing, stricter voices roar into the opening of the tunnel, the voices and outcry moving closer to where I hide. Pivoting, I take several steps away from the entrance, feeling my way deeper into the darkness, keeping the presence of mind to move cautiously by preventing unnecessary noise betraying my position.

Volcano fumes thicken as I distance myself from the voices and venture further into the unknown. My lungs fight against the noxious fumes when I stop to catch my breath, my eyes straining to seek out safe footing in the dark.

In all the excitement, I had forgotten that Annaliese had returned my visor. With shaking hands, I pull it out from under the robe and slide it over my head. I fasten it tightly, sealing my suit before turning on the air scrubber. In seconds, the air clears and my lungs breath relief.

Playing with the light amplifier, I adjust the visor's screen, the shadows of the tunnel retreat. Directly ahead of me, the shaft shrinks. Bending low, I move onward. The man who brought us to the cave had said the tunnels would lead to the lava river. Whether this particular one goes directly to the river, or how far I had to walk, I did not have the chance to ask.

I work my way forward, running my hand along the wall to my left to ensure I remain strictly to the one tunnel. Along the way, I pass several other offshoots that branch in different directions. My thinking is that if all else fails, I can return to the cave by this same path.

I pause and listen for sounds of pursuit. The shouting and yelling fade. Soon, my laboured breath is the only sound accompanying me. In a small alcove, I sit down to plan ahead. What will I do, what are my options?

At first, I convince myself to wait until the guards return to the city and then backtrack to the oil mines and search out the air chute. Thinking that through, I decide against it. Even if the guards aren't watching the mouth of the cave, even if I escaped capture in the mines and climbed the chute, how long could I reasonably last on the surface? I don't have any food, my backpack along with my shovel and heat pods remain on the opposite end of the city, where I first crossed paths with the inhabitants of Adams Mountain.

And what about Annaliese? She and Marcus risked their freedom when they helped me escape from the cages. Could I leave them to their fate? Was it my problem? All I wanted at the moment was to return home.

Feeling the need to move, I wander aimlessly, unable to arrive at a decision, oblivious to the increasing temperatures in the tunnel. A bead of water tickles my spine, my body soaked with sweat. It must be an indication I am near the lava river. I rush ahead.

I move swiftly over the rocky, uneven trail, squeeze around a narrow bend, only to find the route sealed. The rocks are hot to the touch, so I must be close, but I will have to find another tunnel to get there. After backtracking several hundred feet, the tunnel branches off.

My choices don't get easier. If I stray from this tunnel, will I be able to find it again and return to the oil mine? That option would, with luck, at least get me back to the surface and I could leave this nightmare behind.

I hesitate. A raging debate renders me immobile. I think of Annaliese as she fought the guards and recalled the resignation in her voice when her anger cooled. The thought of her cuts through the indecision in my mind. I realize that I have no choice.

I will not leave Annaliese. I will find a way to help her.

My options are not good. If I return to the cave, I am risking inevitable capture. These people know the mines a lot better than I do, so I wouldn't stand much of a chance. No. I will have to walk these tunnels and find a way to the river of red. This same river should run not too far from Adams City.

Easy, I tell myself. All I have to do is navigate these tunnels, walk along the river without getting cooked and then sneak into a fortified city and free Annaliese. What could be simpler? Besides, no matter which course I choose, I figure the outcome is bound to be the same.

It was my life to do with what I needed and at present, I don't picture myself living to old age. So, back to the city it was, then. With the last shred of reservation cast aside, I walk into the new tunnel with renewed determination.

Several hours pass and then another dead end. The volcano shafts are hot, but I keep pushing on. My breathing is laboured as I venture from tunnel to tunnel. At one dead end, the tunnel splits in numerous directions. Weariness beats down on me. I move forward carelessly, a rock rolls under my boot. My feet slip and I slide forward. My boots and then legs pass over the edge of a drop.

Panicked, I twist and swing my arm, reaching for the edge. The fingers of my injured arm catch on the rough rock, shooting jolts of pain spike to my brain. Scrambling to throw my other hand up for support, my fingers slam onto the lip and slide. The rim of the edge slips from my hold and I drop. I fall over backward into a pile of sticks on the floor. I land hard, my head bangs off the rocky floor, the light in my helmet shorts out and I lay in complete blackness. Rising to my knees, I push past the sticks in my path.

The exhaustion of my search and the bruising from my fall settles over me, and I doze off. I am not sure how long I sleep for, but in my dreams, Annaliese is screaming as she falls from the edge of the cliff into the oil mine. I startle awake and sit straight up, looking around. It's too dark to see. My body is saturated inside my thermal suit. My fingers go to my helmet to turn the power on. The switch clicks, but the helmet remains dark.

I vaguely remember falling and my helmet smashing into the floor. Fumbling with my visor, I fail to activate the lighting mechanism. My fingers grope, but are unsuccessful. As a last resort I raise my hand and slap the side of my helmet. Each slap fails to turn on the light. Each time my hand strikes my helmet harder.

The light flickers, than catch. Giving the visor a second to see if the lights will remain shining, I adjust the amplifier and scan around me. Annaliese's fall was a dream. I don't see her around. My eyes pass over bundles of brown rags, white sticks spilling from the cloth and scattered over the floor of the small shaft. I turn my head from the sticks and glance up at the lip of the tunnel above.

It is too far to jump, and the wall is worn smooth. Air pockets riddle the side, each one too small to provide a foot or handhold. Dejectedly, I stare at the wall wondering if this is how my story ends. I curse my stupid luck and lean with my back to the wall, resting.

At least I can start a fire with the sticks, I think and find the irony amusing as the walls of the shaft radiate extreme heat from the volcanic river. My stomach rumbles, reminding me that it has been a while since I last ate.

I pluck a stick from the floor. How would they accumulate in a cavern this far in the tunnels? I study the stick closer. The one I grabbed is a couple of inches around with knobby ends, 12 or 14 inches long...shit, it's not a stick at all, I realize and I open my hand letting, it fall back to the floor.

I look over the littered floor. I am certainly not the first person to be lost in these tunnels. Judging by the amount of bones covering the floor, several people have met their ends in this shaft. Repulsed, I close my eyes to block out the sight.

I lay still for hours, preparing for the end. Don't give up, a little voice in my head pleads. When I have enough of the voice, I stand up. Flashes of me being stranded and dying alone in this maze of tunnels creep into my head, fuelling my resolve to find the lava river.

Unless I can climb the wall, my chances of ever seeing Annaliese again are over. I stare at the wall, at the tiny holes in its face. With no protrusions to aid my climb, nothing short of a ladder would work. A thought floats elusively around my brain, but my depression prevents me from grasping it. Angered, I pick up a bone and smash it into the wall. The bone splinters, the end broken into smaller slivers.

"What is trapped in my head, what should I know?" I yell into the darkness of the pit, the bone still in my hand. My eyes fall to the end of the splinter bone and the elusive thought surfaces. I jab the splintered bone into one of the holes on the face of the drop and remove my hand. The bone sticks out of the rock.

I look back over the scattered bones and, repulsed by what I am about to do, I start fashioning the bones to fill the holes and provide a way out. The day passes; I spend hours breaking and grinding a ladder provided by the people who died in this shaft before me. My first few attempts fall short, but determined to escape, I surge on.

Gripping the rim with my fingers, I drag my body and then my legs over the top. Resting in the tunnel, my thoughts return into the shaft, my head dipped in thanks to the dead for their sacrifice.

For the next two days, I scramble in and out the tunnels, hunting for an opening to the river. Some tunnels were stifling with heat; others are cool, even cold, to the touch.

Thirsty and starving, I stumble through yet another endless tunnel. The temperature increases as I walk, but I don't get too excited. I have been down this path of hope before. The floor is treacherous; I make my way around another bend.

Light. A glow of red rises in the distance ahead of me. Reaching deep inside my soul, I find a resurgence of will and stagger forward. The heat intensifies as I approach the end of my search.

Slowly, I creep close to the tunnel opening, wary not to stumble. Loose rocks litter the mouth of the tunnel spilling over the edge. Leaning over, my upper body balanced by my hands propped on my knees, I peer out over the river of red, sweat dripping onto the screen of my visor.

About 20 below the mouth of the tunnel runs a shallow stream of liquefied red rock flowing by the bottom of the canyon wall, the heat of the river pouring into the tunnel opening. My body is exhausted from several days of wandering, but my hopes are high. Not far from this cave mouth should lay the shiny city.

A short drop from the lip of the tunnel is a ledge that juts out and runs alongside the canyon wall, parallel to the flowing river of molten rock. I turn and lower my legs over the jagged edge. Nervously, I ease my body over the edge until I am holding on with only my fingers, pain reminding me of my injured arm. I take a couple of deep breaths, and with a little prayer, I let go. The drop is farther than it looks.

I land awkwardly and as I clamber to gain my balance, the side of the ledge crumbles, my foot slips. The force of my body drives my knees hard onto the ledge. Rocks tear into my suit. Instinctively, I roll onto my backside dragging my foot back onto the precarious shelf that sits only feet above the heat and certain death the passing river presents.

My heart beats rapidly in my chest. Through my open mouth, I gulp in the stale air inside my visor. I don't pause long. The heat from the river is intense. My dehydrated, weary body does not need much of an excuse to surrender.

Swinging my head from side to side to check my surroundings, I try to orient myself in the direction of the city. A wrong guess and my chances diminish. Right, I decide, the city has to be to the right of my position. Don't ask me how I know, but years guiding the ice sled across the frozen surface of this planet have instilled a sense of direction that I have learned to trust.

Standing on the precarious ledge, I cling to the uneven cliff wall and carefully I move. The lighting provided by my visor, along with the glow of the heated lava provides me with enough light to see. At times, the better light is almost a curse, as the ledge gets very narrow in spots before it once again grows wider. Along the path, the rocky outcropping dips to down within inches of the flowing river and then climbs back high above it.

Everywhere I look, towering walls formed from age-old solidified lava rise. The river is nothing more than a trickle in a vast canyon that has been shaped by the lava over hundreds of years of volcanic activity.

My strength and hope dwindle as I fall into the routine of robotically sliding one foot after the other. I feel like I am being cooked alive inside my suit, but surely without the suit and my visor, I would have been long dead from the unbearable heat and the deadly fumes drifting up from below.

One more step, one more bend to climb around, I keep telling myself. I slide up to a protrusion blocking my path. The ledge is almost non-existent now. With my hand, I feel for anything to hold on to as I edge very hesitantly around the obstacle.

A few times, I lose my footing as I gingerly place my feet. With a death grip, I cling to the wall. The fear of falling into the heated river below never leaves my mind. Nearing the end of the bend, the ledge widens once more and with quicker steps I scramble to a more secure footing.

I suck in mouthfuls of air and steady myself, my body shivers, whether from exhaustion or fear, I don't know. The excruciating pain from my arm aches on. Supporting my weight with my hands on my knees, I rest, probably longer than I think and with a final shove of determination I straighten up. The outcropping I am standing on is wide enough for me to turn around.

I pull my gaze away from the ledge I had just climbed over and look past the protrusion. High above me, the shadows in the cavern are fainter, almost like...like the glow from artificial light is warding them off. I chance a smile and my hopes lift...if I am not mistaking, the city is not far off.

Chapter 19

Enter The City

A surge of energy pulses through my blood, my hunger and thirst pushed aside. Letting my eyes travel the length of the wall in front of me, I search for a series of hand and foot holds that I can use to climb away from the heat of the river.

The fingers of my right hand secure a firm grip on a pocket in the cooled rock. I raise one foot onto a broken ledge and begin my climb. Swinging my left hand up, I aim for a protrusion above my head. Closing my hand, I test the strength of my injured arm before sliding my other foot higher on the wall. Pain travels the nerves, but I hold on long enough to raise myself and I start over. Hand, foot, and then my other hand, and with it come tears of pain. Then finally my last foot and repeat.

I cling to the wall of rock and work my way upward. The climb is not that great, but the last couple of days have left me weak. The lack of food and water force me to creep along so slowly that the climb takes hours. My breaks become longer and the time I spend climbing grows shorter. Every movement is a battle to get my fatigued body to respond until the top looms within reach. I tell myself that all I need is a moment to rest. The past few days have taken their toll, leaving me weaker than I'll admit.

With a struggle, my head crests the lip of the cliff.

Keeping very still, I scan the shadows close to the edge where I hang. I can't see the bright lights of the city, but the darkness on this higher level isn't as void of light as the area where I had first fallen from the ice cave. My best guess puts me about halfway between the rocks where I met the guards and the city itself.

Pulling my body over the lip of the cliff, I take time to study the cavern around me. I can't risk being discovered by guards patrolling the lava field. Turning my back to the direction of the city, I move with my body close to the ground using outcroppings of rock as cover while I walk away from the river's edge and closer to the spot where I left my supplies.

The cavern grows darker as I search. The surroundings begin to look familiar; I notice the landmark I made note of the day I fell captive, what now seems like an eternity. I comb the rocks and shadows, scouring the area until I locate my backpack. It lies undisturbed exactly where I left it those many days ago. Stuffing the pack under my arm, I climb in search of ice that accumulates away from the heat of the river.

Moving warily through the lava fields, I avoid the trail dashing between cover to remain hidden. The temperature falls as the distance from the river increases, providing a welcome relief. Before long, the light of my visor falls over drifts of ice. I touch the frozen water, never happier to see ice and feel the cold radiate from it.

Ripping off my visor, I chip ice into a cup and set it over a heat pod. My mouth is parched. Impatiently, I watch the ice in the cup and wait for the soothing relief I know the water will bring. Sticking loose chips of ice in my mouth, I dig inside my pack for a container of food. I prepare the finest meal I have ever eaten and follow it up with a sip of melted ice.

The water burns as it trickles down my constricted throat. I sip small amounts of water, my throat raw and swollen from the dehydration of the past few days. Mixing the water with small mouthfuls of food, I lay back and revel in the coolness of the ice banks.

A day passes as I recover, and with my limited knowledge of the city's layout, I devise a plan to free Annaliese. Near the end of the second day, I'm well enough to move. Stuffing supplies in different pockets of my suit, I hide my pack in the crook of a rock pile. Leaving the comfort of the ice, I weave my way back among the tangle of rocks toward the City of Adams Mountain.

The easiest way in is straight down the path I had first walked. The closer I get to the shining lights, the more I think about my plan. I decide to use a less direct route, taking advantage of the littered grounds of volcanic debris that line the sides of the trail.

A safe distance from the city, I climb to my right and into a field strewn with boulders. The route I have decided on will take me over and around mounds and large crags, but it will provide me with the best cover. My progress is slow and deliberate, because if I misjudge my footing, I can look forward to a body's worth of broken bones.

When the outline of the city is in sight, I hide among a cluster of rocks. Removing my helmet, I fold and fasten it to the back of my suit. The lights of the city are dim. I rest and watch the buildings bordering the edge of the lava field. I place my trust in Marcus' description of life in the city. Banking on the curfew and the lack of civilians on the streets at this hour, the number of eyes that could spot my return should be reduced

I creep into a deserted section, several blocks north of the building that houses the cages. My plan is more random than premeditated. The start of it is simple. Find a lone guard, subdue him and then force him to tell me where they are holding Annaliese.

I move in the shadows of the streets and alleys until I locate a pair of guards walking their rounds close to where I entered. So far on my journey into the city, I have spotted random pairings of guards. But because of logistics, I decide to follow these two. Mirroring their movements, I slip from shadow to shadow, waiting for an opportune time to ambush them. A pattern in their routine develops. The two don't venture far in their travels, so the three of us circle while I wait to spring a trap.

The men stop at the mouth of an alley. Creeping behind a pile of refuse, I watch and wait. One of the guards leaves his partner and retraces his steps back into the alley. His walk brings him close to where I hide.

Worming tighter between the pile and a wall, I crouch low to the ground, hoping my presence goes unnoticed. The man walks past me to a break between buildings, his back turned to me while he stops and relieves himself. I glance back in the direction of the second guard. The man is facing away from his partner. The pile of scrap blocks the line of sight between the two men.

Seizing the opportunity, I grab a scrap of iron and tip toe softly toward the preoccupied guard. Within a few steps of the man I straighten to my full height, the piece of metal raised above my head. I am almost directly behind the man when he starts to turn.

I swing viciously, the metal cutting a path downward at the man's head. A startled grunt escapes his throat as the metal smashes with the side of his face. Bones crunch under the force of my swing. The guard crumples to the ground. I swing the metal a second time before I drop it and rush to remove the man's uniform. My mind screams for me to hurry before his partner comes to investigate.

Rolling and tugging, I free the robe and pull it over my shoulders covering my thermal suit. I bend and retrieve the man's rifle, then pause to slow my heart rate and recoup my strength. With a shaky confidence, I stride toward the mouth of the alley, closing the distance to the second guard.

The man standing patrol near the opening moves his head aware of the sound of my footsteps. He speaks to me over his shoulder. Mumbling a reply, I cough to disguise my voice and pull the robe's hood lower over my face.

Fear and tension increase the pounding of my heart. I step closer to the second guard. The man casually turns and looks directly at me. I am still yards away from the mouth of the alley. I keep my head tilted down, my face shaded by the hood, but I watch the man study me. His confusion delays his reaction. The barrel of my rifle swings settling on his chest.

"Drop your gun," I bark and motion into the alley.

His rifle clatters to the street. The guard's eyes narrow at me, still, he obeys. Stepping behind the man, I dig the barrel of the gun into his back to prod him along. I bend to scoop up his discarded firearm and follow silently behind him, the two of us travelling deeper into the alley. At the break in the buildings where his partner is lying unconscious, I command the guard to stop.

"Grab his feet and drag him behind those bins," I instruct, using the gun to point to the stacks against the wall. Nervously, I glance around and follow the two until we are out of sight.

"Where is Annaliese?" I ask. The guard looks at me dumbfounded.

"Annaliese," I repeat. "The High Prophet's daughter." Still, the man stares at me like I speak a different language. I'm not sure what to do; I have never had to question anyone before. The guard's blank eyes study me as he continues to ignore my question.

My hand goes under the hood of the robe, my fingers scratching my scalp. The guard seizes the opportunity and steps toward me. I hesitate and he rushes grabbing for the gun. I hold on tight with all my strength as he tries to wrestle the rifle free.

He lifts his foot to kick me. I turn, the blow glances off the side of my leg. A surge of anger mixed with fear steels my determination. I jerk the gun close to my body, pulling the guard off balance. His head snaps toward me. Twisting the rifle across my body, I drive my elbow into the side of his face.

The blow stuns the guard. With the momentum returning in my favour, I knock him off balance pushing him back into the stacked bins and follow with my shoulder into his stomach. The air rushes from his mouth, he grasp on the rifle eases. I yank hard, pulling it from his grip. At the same time, I sweep my foot behind his legs, tripping him and send him tumbling backwards.

He falls hard into the building. I pounce on top of him and smash the butt of the gun down on his head and shoulder repeatedly. Three times I do this until I can quell the anger burning inside. The guard lays crumpled on the ground, his breathing ragged.

"Where is Annaliese?" I ask again, my voice harsh with anger.

"Locked in her room. In the Prophet's house," he answers, his face bloody and broken

"How do I find this house?" The guard hesitates for a moment. His eyes fill with fear as I raise the gun ready to strike him another blow. His voice quivers as he coughs up the directions. "I hope you're successful." He mumbles seconds before my rifle crashes into his head.

The guard's words ring in my head as I rip apart his robe binding the unconscious men.

Chapter 20

Change Of Plans

The night passes by too quickly. I have lost time by slipping into the city and tracking the guards and morning can't be far away. I am at the point of no return. The layout of the city streets is foreign to me and that adds to my slow progress. Caution is pushed aside for distance. Sticking to the alleys and dark shadows, I skirt the main streets in my search of the High Prophet's house.

Annaliese had described her house to me when we first met, so at every cross street I stop and study the rooflines. She said it was the biggest house in the city. House being the key word, not building, and that coupled with the guard's directions narrows my search.

At one such street crossing, I look one way then the other. The road runs straight in both directions. At the far end of a long block, I spot a roof and upper windows of what I would classify a large house.

The sight of the structure is encouraging and I advance, stepping blindly out of the mouth of the alley. A blow strikes my face and sends me stumbling. Bursts of light explode in my skull.

Dazed, I violently shake off the effects, the thought of failing Annaliese burn in my soul. "You're no help to her if you're captured," a voice in my head yells. I prepare to fight my way free as my vision clears. I find myself surrounded by a band of guards.

One of the men squats down beside me, his hand lifting the hood, revealing my face. His words mix with the ringing in my ears.

"Sorry," Marcus apologizes. "You startled us when you stepped around the corner. We had heard that you entered the city, but when we lost sight of you we set out scouring the streets to find you."

I sit up and rub my jaw staring into Marcus' face, my eyes still tearing from the blow to the head.

"I don't understand," I say, "Annaliese and I were certain that the guards would have captured you after you led them away the door at the mine."

Marcus shakes his head. "It's a long story, one for another time. I can only presume that if you are foolish enough to return to the city you must have a good reason."

"Annaliese. I came back to help her."

Marcus nods. "When I heard that you returned I figured she might be the reason. I put out the word and sent people to intercept you."

"What are your plans?" He asks.

I shrug my shoulders. "Find Annaliese and get her out of the city."

Marcus looks at me thoughtfully. "That is not much of a plan." He stands up and offers me his hand. Climbing to my feet, I dust my clothing off. I stall for time thinking about his reaction. How well do I know him, how far can I trust him? I wonder if it's not odd that he and his gang are roaming the streets with all the guards patrolling. I look past him at the other men. Each and everyone including Marcus are wearing the camouflage uniforms of the city guards. Something serious must be going down for a group of this size to be risking curfew.

"What's happening?" I motion to his men. "Why are the bunch of you willing to risk arrest?"

His face darkens, and he lowers his head. "Annaliese will be tried before the council later today. Nobody expects the trial to last long and people fear that the prophets will be exceedingly harsh with her punishment. We are going to stop the trial."

"How?" I ask puzzled. "You don't have very many men."

"More than you think." He raises his head. "Annaliese is well liked and respected through out the city. She has touched a lot of people with her kindness and charity." He smiles at the thought. "News of her arrest has stirred feelings of anger. The rumour of her treatment has caused a rift among the city. Comes a time when a feared leader oversteps his boundaries. The time is now."

Clouds of guilt descend on me while I listen to Marcus, because the trouble brewing in the shiny city and Annaliese's arrest are my fault. Her act of kindness toward me may break the city into fragments. I can't be responsible for ruining the lives of so many. The path I must take is clear.

I express my concerns to Marcus. His men stare at me, wondering about my sanity, I presume. "I will turn myself in, trade my freedom for hers," I decide. "I can make a deal with the prophets."

"That won't happen. The prophets won't bargain. Their control over the city is fragile at best. If they soften their stand, that will only weaken their authority."

I kick at the dirt in frustration. "Then we will have to storm the palace and release her, what other option do we have?"

"We will never get close. The palace is under heavy guard and even though portions of the guards are sympathetic to Annaliese, the ones protecting the High Prophet's house are his most loyal."

"Then what do we do?" My voice rises in desperation. I worry that the hour is late, and the lights of the city will surely be brightening soon. At any moment, people will awaken and leave their homes for the start of a new day. How will we have any chance with so many more obstacles in the way of our already impossible task?

"Where will her trial be held and how many guards will be there?" I ask Marcus, searching for some sliver of hope. An idea worms its way into my head. The thought seems crazy, even to me, but under the circumstances, crazy may be what we need.

"The trial will convene on the palace steps." Marcus eyes me apprehensively. "A squad of palace guards accompany the prophets and without a doubt, several more troops will be stationed in the streets watching the crowds." Squatting down, Marcus draws a rough sketch in the dust, lines and squares depicting the streets and palace to illustrate his words. Twisting his head, he peers back up at me. "Why. What are you thinking?"

Standing among the group of men, I grasp at straws, stringing fragments of random thoughts together in the form of a plan. The words tumble out of my mouth as I think out loud. The variables are many and the time is short. Marcus picks up on my train of thought, and together we arrive at a possible plan of attack.

Marcus informs me that there are more insurgents he will call on to assist. We decide that I will lead a small mob of men to the steps of the palace before the trial, and try to delay the proceedings. Marcus has preparations of his own to complete, but has assured me that he will send more sympathizers to aid in our task.

"The trial will take place on the steps of the palace at first light. Wait here until the crowds gather." Marcus instructs as he selects a few of the men to stay with me. The remainder will travel with him. "That should allow me time to alert the others and have them meet you here before the trial begins."

He takes me aside to talk. "The resentment in the city is running high right now. The people of Adams Mountain tire of the prophet's rule and are shocked that Annaliese will be tried. Although most will be sympathetic, the majority, even if they have come to despise the prophets, are too afraid to act and out of fear will stand against us," he warns. "Careful of who you turn your back on in trust." He pats my shoulder and walks out of the alley.

I find myself alone with four of Marcus' men. We seek refuge in the remaining shadows of the buildings and bide our time. The last remaining hours of darkness slowly pass while we wait for the city lights to brighten. Through the hours, stragglers sent by Marcus appear out of the darkened streets to bolster our small band.

By the time the city is about to wake, our little gathering is a mere 15 people. A few in our group have military robes and rifles; the others are garbed in regular clothes.

Our wait draws to an end. The city powers up, and the streets become bathed in daylight. A bell resonates throughout the streets. One of Marcus' men interrupts my thoughts and nods toward the palace.

I study the faces of the small group assembled around me. The people are scared and nervous. I don't blame them. I step in front as we leave the sanctuary of the alley toward the palace steps.

Annaliese's trial is about to start.

Chapter 21

Annaliese's Trial

Parents with children in hand leave their houses and walk with other families, small clusters of individuals pour from the doors of buildings and out of side alleys as we pass joining the exodus to the palace. The crowds thicken as we walk the final blocks.

The ringing of footsteps and muffled conversations reverberate down the main street long before we catch sight of the multitudes already gathered for the trial. A block away from the palace steps, the flow of new arrivals begins to converge into the square, choking the street, forcing us to slow our walk. I keep my eyes busy, roaming over the heads of the town people and watch the surrounding streets.

What had started out a couple blocks back consisting of a few random individuals has quickly ballooned into swelling numbers as more men and women add to the gathering and the walk to palace steps.

The merging of the population of Adams Mountain masks our arrival. Working deep into the crowd, I wonder about our plan. The odds are enormous. Each of the men who have followed me is painfully aware of the impossibility of the task ahead. Being in the midst of this sea of people, the size of our small band of dissenters feels even more diminutive.

I move among the crowd and study their faces. Will any of these men and women rise to help us once we make our move, or will their fear of the prophets' force them to stand against us? I search for a way to disrupt Annaliese's trial until Marcus returns, if he returns at all. Our hastily devised plan contains many flaws, and even if everything goes in our favour what chance do the few of us have compared to the trained guards of the prophets?

A hush falls over the crowd. I turn my attention to the palace steps. A double line of guards, draped in blue camouflage uniforms, leads a procession out of a set of ornate wooden doors. Close on their heels walk four colourfully robed prophets. The succession of guards part at a dais centered at the edge of the palace steps. The prophets stop a few paces behind.

The murmuring and jostling from the growing crowd falls silent. My heart begins to race, my eyes locked on the open door in anticipation. I can't help but think if it weren't for me, Annaliese would not be in this position.

Whispered cries of disbelief and anger ruminate at the sight of Annaliese escorted from the palace. Her head is held high beneath the hood of her robe. Resignation and surrender mask her face, but she stares beyond the dais and out into the milling crowd.

Close on her heels walks another prophet, this one adorned in robes of a more intricate design and bolder colours. I assume he must be the High Prophet, but I refrain from asking the people around me for fear of drawing unwanted attention.

People begin to grow restless; whispers of disapproval and even outrage ripple through the gathered masses, rising in intensity. I glance around the fringes of the packed street; men in military robes push into the sea of bodies searching for the more boisterous protests.

My attention swings back to the scene on the front steps. The growing rumblings from the street drown out the High Prophet's opening statement. Although I cannot hear his words, I can see him pause, allowing the noise from the crowd to subside.

"We, the humble servants of your great city, stand before you with great displeasure today," he announces. "The treachery of a dear and respected member of this community has betrayed your confidence and her treachery weighs heavy on my heart." The Prophet shifts his gaze to Annaliese before resuming his speech.

"We, the prophets of Adams Mountain, have devoted our lives for the well-being of all the citizens of this city, only to be blindsided by the one person we felt was beyond corruption and a true believer of our faith."

The Prophet's voice increases in volume and conviction. His words speak of the unselfish sacrifices of the ruling class and the tough decisions they have made for the prosperity of the city. He reminds the crowd of how his ancestors had founded the city and fought to provide a refuge in an effort to avoid prosecution from the outside world.

He speaks of how the original prophets and their followers were falsely persecuted for actions that led to the disruption of the earth's climate. How, during the climate wars, the prophet's forefathers faced down the leagues of deniers, risking all to save humanity by promoting the innovations of clean energy alternatives to prevent further destruction of a fragile environment devastated by the use of fossil fuels.

The High Prophet banged the dais when he talked about the 21st century deniers and their claims that the vibrations from the forests of turbines were believed to have shaken the earth's core, resulting in the eruptions of volcanoes. Not true, the High Prophet preached. The reckless harvest and exploitation of oil products by blind governments and greedy energy barons and the addictions of an ignorant population to the dirty fuels were to blame for the catastrophe, he said.

When the volcanoes spewed the ash and dust high into the atmosphere, thus blocking the life-sustaining rays of the sun from reaching earth's surface, the panicked governments turned on the saviours of the planet as convenient scapegoats. Lies, he drones on, untruths meant to divert the blame and punish the environmental faithful, the only people who were truly defending the helpless planet. Our founder learned not to trust outsiders and now, after nearly two centuries of suffering and hiding, we find that we face the same ongoing problems.

While the Prophet's sermon of treachery and sacrifice stream from the raised palace steps and over the crowd, I busy myself studying the streets and alleys surrounding the square at the front steps of the palace. When will Marcus appear? I wonder, and with how many others? The military guards interspersed throughout the crowd and along the streets are now many more compared to the small band of Marcus' men who ventured into the crowd with me.

The High Prophet's voice calms; his speech sounds like it is winding down. Then what? The Prophet speaks to the people of Adams Mountain about the planet's unforgiving surface, the roaming bands of criminals and how the city is in constant danger brought by the harbingers of death in the form of outsiders.

This statement catches my attention. I have travelled the surface above this hidden city for years, and never once came across any bands of armed men roaming the deserts of snow. In fact, I have rarely ever noticed tracks from movement aside from our own and knew damn well the people of the New Capital had no intention of ever attacking anyone.

Hell. We had no idea this place even existed. It is apparent that the prophets use their people's ignorance of the outside world to spread fear with misinformation to allow them to maintain a tight grip on power. Combined with the promise of a life toiling in the oil mines for anybody who dares challenge their authority, the Prophets have elevated their status to a divine right.

The High Prophet ends his propaganda-raged speech to a smattering of applause. The anger that had contorted his face during his rant changes slowly to a look of sadness and disappointment. He pauses dramatically then reads the charges against his daughter, Annaliese.

"With much reservation, the council finds Annaliese Sento guilty of treachery and colluding with the enemy against the safety of Adams Mountain. There is also a second charge of aiding and abetting a known enemy and her assistance in his plot to exploit our defences." The High Prophet lowers his head in sorrow and lets his words settle over the surprised and puzzled crowd. "The council finds that your betrayal was meant for one purpose only," the Prophet emphasizes as his fist pounds the lectern. "To assist our enemies with their desire to conquer this city and enslave its people!"

The mood of the crowd shifts, first from the sympathy they displayed upon Annaliese's arrival on the palace steps to rumblings of disbelief and shock, and then finally to outrage.

My anger rises at the flood of lies that Annaliese's father apparently has little or no remorse in fabricating. The thought that this man was more than willing to sacrifice his daughter so easily for power made my blood boil.

"The punishment for such treachery will be dealt with harshly and quickly. The council has chosen a fitting penalty as an example to others who think of undermining the fabric of Adams Mountain. No one is above the laws of this city, not even you, daughter."

"Don't you mean your arcane prophet laws," comes a loud cry from the packed street. Ripples of dissension echo through the audience, rebellious voices join in chorus. The High Prophet looks out over the crowd in the general direction of the outburst and nods his head. Guards dispersed among the crowd push toward the voices. I notice people glancing at me and am reminded of the guard uniform I am wearing. I shrug off the looks and return my attention to the palace steps.

The Prophet watches the action briefly. He turns to face Annaliese. "For your acts of treason, daughter, the council has ruled to banish you to the surface. You will be provided with supplies and your own devices for survival," he announces. "This sentence is to be carried out immediately." The High Prophet takes a few steps away from Annaliese and motions for the guards to seize her.

The reading of the charges and then the excessive sentence stun me. Annaliese will not last more than hours on the frozen surface. I refuse to let her suffer for the kindness she had shown me. Her only crime was being sympathetic.

I grip the rifle hanging by my side and then pat the reading paper hidden under my robe. I need to convince the good people of Adams Mountain that they are being misled and manipulated by these self-proclaimed prophets.

My time is short. In desperation, I cast about for signs of Marcus and the help he promised. I have never considered myself a hero, but damned if I was going to stand by while Annaliese's life was forfeited solely for the Prophet's propaganda.

I have no idea of what type of delay I can provide, but that doesn't stop me. I grip my rifle tighter. I feel a hand fleetingly pull at my robe. Glancing at the man beside me, I see his hand quickly retract, one of Marcus' men trying to caution me. I ignore the warning. With a shove, I start to shoulder my way through the anxious and confused crowd toward the steps and

Annaliese, damned if I will let anyone banish her to the surface.

Chapter 22

Confronting The Madness

At first, my moving toward the palace steps surprises the people close to me, but then they start moving aside and allow me to pass. It takes a second to understand before I realize it is because of the camouflage robe I am wearing.

The men and women between the palace steps and where I move must believe that I am to assist in the transport of the prisoner. I stand tall, tug the fabric of the robe's hood lower and walk for the steps, the rifle clutched at my side. How close can I get to Annaliese before being discovered remains to be determined?

Nearing the leading edge of the crowd stands a barrier of guards posted to separate the crowd in the street and the prophets on the steps. One of the men looks me in the eye as I approach. I return his stare with a passive face; the fear I'm feeling I hide deep inside.

I take another step. Another guard looks at me quizzically. The first guard raises a hand to halt me. I nod at the man and take another step. Undecided, his hand flinches for his rifle.

Twisting the gun in my hand, I drive the metal butt into his stomach.

I step around the crumpled guard and point my rifle. The barrel trained on the High Prophet.

"Run," I holler at Annaliese. She stands motionless, her eyes a mixture of astonishment and fear. "Run," I repeat switching my attention back to the High Prophet. The barrel of the rifle unwavering as I keep it locked on the leader of Adams Mountain.

In a barely audible voice, Annaliese looks down the steps at me. "No," she replies. My focus remains on the High Prophet, but I stop my advance.

"You shouldn't have come," Annaliese cries out. The quiet words just leave her mouth when a new sound fills the air. The sound of rifles being raised followed by the actions of bullets sliding into empty chambers.

The Prophet's guards block my path, their guns aimed in my direction. Looking around, I notice more guards with rifles pointed across the steps at me.

"Let her go and I will surrender," I shout at Annaliese's father. From within the shadow of his robe's hood, a sneer moves the man's lips.

"I don't think so." The words boom out of his mouth while he gazes down at me. "Set down your gun, you fool." He gestures with his hand toward the guards. "Your little charade is over. Take him!" He instructs his palace guards and grabs Annaliese by the arm and turns.

Before anyone moves, some of the guards standing on the steps pull the hoods off their heads and swivel the guns they hold sideways to cover the remaining guards in the front line. One of the disobedient guards smiles as he glances at me. It's the same young man who had days before rushed into the hidden room to warn us.

The crowd quiets mesmerized by the scene unfolding on the palace steps. Then some jostling and shouts come from behind me. The small band of men Marcus sent to assist me shove past stunned onlookers and walk toward the steps. The guns they carry brandished in defiance of the prophets and their authority.

The High Prophet screams for reinforcements, his voice high and strained. His passive face reddens; his composure stripped bare revealing cracks in his façade. Incredulity, fear twists his facial features as he watches the beginning of revolt on the steps of the palace.

"Stop them," he yells, his head swinging from side to side, his smouldering darks eyes darting frantically about the street. His expression changes from confusion to rage and fury. "Stop them now!" he bellows at his guards. Blasts from a siren wail adding to the chaos, the shrill whine echoing above the growing commotion.

The warnings of the sirens bring more guards rushing into the jammed streets leading into the palace square. I hold my position on the steps, captivated by the sudden flurry of motion.

I am afraid that the few soldiers with me will not stand much of a chance against the trained military guards. Despondent, I watch the number of guards multiply. Fortunately for us, the reinforcements will have to contend with the mass of bodies packing the street, the guards bound to waste time fighting a way through to reach our location. On some fronts, the crowds part, allowing the guards an easy passage. In other areas, the townsfolk stand firm and hamper the advancement of the Prophet's men.

The reinforcements wade into the midst of the crowded street before the improbable happens. The sea of bodies ebbs and flows beckoning the soldiers into the middle of the foray. Then, by some unspoken command, the men and women of the angry crowd close ranks, trapping the unsuspecting men. The crowd has the troops surrounded.

The High Prophet shouts words of anger from the steps as he watches the large crowd immobilize his troops.

"Shoot...shoot anyone and everyone in your way!" He bellows from the steps. His high-pitched voice carries over the bedlam. The brash show of defiance by the very people he lords over adding a sense of alarm to his screams.

Suddenly, a scene of unmitigated horror ensues.

The trapped guards use their rifles as clubs swinging to clear a path; others hindered by the crush of bodies heed the Prophet's order to fire their guns into the shocked citizens of Adams Mountain. The advantage goes from the crowd to the armed soldiers. The mob of people recoils at the sound of gunfire and the screams of their neighbours.

Standing on the palace steps, I watch dumbfounded at the horror playing out on the street below. Adding to the melee, a second roar of gunfire echoes off the buildings. My eyes search over the chaos for its source.

Entering from a side street into the square, Marcus leads a horde of grime-covered miners and marches into the fray on the already packed street, the rifles they carry blasting shots above the crowd. Marcus works the lever on his gun; the barrel pointed high into the air as he fires warning shots to distract the soldiers.

He continues walking into the confused crowd leading the miners. The miners with their tattered robes and grimy faces push through the wall of bodies, eager to combat the trapped guards.

Annaliese's screams wrench my focus back to the steps. Her father has her tight in his grip and is pulling her toward the palace doors. The High Prophet is ranting like a lunatic; his screams of anger to the palace guards mix with Annaliese's cries of fright.

I race up the steps. The colourfully robed prophets guess my intention and move to stop me. Never have I felt the need to hurt another human before. An evil smile grows on my face as I continue forward to meet the challenge. Unused to physically dealing with people, the prophets move awkwardly. What they lack in experience, they mask with numbers.

The first one falls to the butt of my rifle. A second Prophet latches onto my injured arm. I howl in pain and start lashing and hammering in anger, the butt of my gun cutting recklessly through the air. The prophets' determination to stop me is formidable but the rage coursing in my blood says otherwise.

For minutes, the prophets hold my attention, but Annaliese's screams ring across the steps. I swing and strike harsher as her cries pull me forward. Sweat drips off my body by the time I knock the last prophet to the ground.

A door slams shut as I step over the bodies of the High Prophet's henchmen. I lift my head and search for Annaliese. The large, heavy doors of the palace entrance hide her. Rushing to the doors, I yank on the handles. It is locked.

I hustle from the doors and race to a window, the butt of my rifle raised and ready. I smash the gun against the window; shards of glass fly and fall across the floor of the palace. I climb into the opening.

A sliver of glass still embedded in the window frame slices deep into my thigh as my foot touches the floor. Straightening up, I find myself alone in a large foyer. Inside the house, I hear a scream echo. Clutching the rifle in one hand, I use my other hand to stem the bleeding in my leg. The warm, sticky liquid oozes past my fingers, leaving a bloody trail of footprints following me across the room.

Another scream replaces the worry of the blood leaking from my wound off my mind, and I push further into the palace. My adrenaline rises with every beat of my heart. The exertion from walking increases the blood flowing from my wound, the leg of my suit stained. Crossing from the front and around a staircase, I limp into a hallway.

The walled tunnel leads toward the back of the house. Footsteps ring across the floor deeper in the palace, a door slams, and the hallway bends. I come face to face with a faded wooden door. I try the doorknob. It resists turning. Annaliese's muffled screams rise from behind the locked door.

I take a step back and then throw the weight of my body into the door. It doesn't budge. I try again. Same result. My head reels from the loss of blood pulsing from my wound, my actions turn sluggish. Stopping to suck air into my lungs, I fish for a solution to allow me past the door. Another scream.

An idea crests my dulled state of mind. I look from my rifle to the doorknob. Raising the rifle high, with all my strength I drive the metal stock into the doorknob. The knob and rifle butt break on contact. The door swings inward, revealing a staircase. The stairs lead down to a dimly lit landing.

My breathing is growing ragged and the haziness in my head threatens to overcome me. Grabbing hold of the handrail, I hobble down the stairs, dragging my wounded leg over the steps.

Another defiant cry from Annaliese and then hearing her plead and shout I shrug off the pain and quicken the speed as I descent. The lower I climb, the dimmer the light, the thicker the fog in my brain. I miss the last step, the weight of my body supported by my wounded leg. A stream of pain radiates from the wound; the shock briefly clears the mist in my head.

Through a haze, I see the shaded outlines of Annaliese and her father. The High Prophet's back is toward me. Annaliese is struggling to break free of his grip. I rush forward.

Within reach of the High Prophet, he turns and glares at me, his face twisted in a mask of hatred. Without thinking, I lurch at him. My wounded leg gives out and the floor rushes up to meet me. I feel the Prophet's boot contact my side. The blow is crushing. I roll away. A couple more severe kicks thud into my body. Stars mix with the haze in my head.

Through misted eyes, I watch the High Prophet. He moves to stand over me, a long handled shovel clutched in his hands. He prepares to end our battle. His lips move, but his voice doesn't penetrate the fog in my brain. A grin of pure evil touches his lips as he prepares to strike. I pull my arms up to protect my head.

Before the Prophet has the opportunity to smash the shovel down on me, the features of his face change again. His mouth forms an O, and his eyes bulge as confusion replaces the anger on his face. The colourfully robed leader of the shiny city staggers, his knees sag and he tumbles in my direction. I roll out of his path and look up. Standing where the High Prophet had last been is Annaliese. Ropes bound around her wrists, a long knife with blood dripping off the blade clutched in her hands.

She kneels beside me. Her tears mix with the dust in the room. I whisper to her.

"I'm sorry," I gaze deep into her eyes. "If it wasn't for me none of this would have happened."

She brushes her hand across my face. A tear runs down her cheek and lands on me. She attempts to smile.

"It was a long time coming. Your being here was only the catalyst."

Epilogue

The last time anyone has seen the prophets in Adams Mountain is well over a year ago. Annaliese and Marcus have accepted the duties of running the city. The task of dealing with the overthrown rulers fell upon Marcus' shoulders, so with a group of volunteers, he escorted the prophets from the city a few days after Annaliese's trial.

In keeping with the wishes of the residents of the city, it was decided that no trial would be forthcoming for the High Prophet and his four cohorts. Instead of confinement, a public opinion favoured the prophets' banishment.

Marcus led the group marching the prophets away from Adams Mountain for a final time. Word of the prophets' fate after leaving the city remains a mystery. Not one of the volunteers, or Marcus for that matter, has yet to reveal what became of the expelled leaders.

Some speculate that the prophets were released deep into the labyrinth of lava tunnels; others believe that the tyrants were walked to a ledge high over the red river and left little choice but to jump. In any regards, the tyrants have faded from the memories of the town collective and have not been back to impose their archaic rules over the once-oppressed inhabitants of Adams Mountain.

A few months after the palace battle, I convinced Annaliese and Marcus to lend me a vehicle and loaded it with supplies for the people of the New Capital. Adams City has modern technology that could aid the lives of those struggling to survive deep beneath the surface in other parts of this cold, miserable planet.

Together, we have formed exploration crews and continue to send voyages to the surface in search of other desolate colonies and to provide help to those who are in need.

We know that it will take years to reach most of the buried communities struggling to endure on this inhospitable planet, but we have made it our mission to deliver the knowledge and machinery that will help the remaining population fight their way back out of the stone ages.

The oil mines are no longer a form of punishment. As for the life-sustaining liquid buried deep inside the earth, we now revere its use like I believe it once was by mankind centuries ago, when people lived and thrived on the surface of the earth.

We erected a monument with the names engraved upon it of all the people forced to death working in the pits. Many times, I have stood in front of this wall staring at my father's name. Paul W. Ryan – Ice Racer.

I have settled into life in Adams Mountain now. There was no reason for my return to the New Capital. All the people there who I had cared for were no longer alive. Here, Annaliese and I have started a new life together. To this day, I still like to wander throughout the city and marvel at its ingenuity and luxuries that I had no idea existed for the majority of my life. I spend my time roaming the streets and talking with people on my journeys.

One of my favourite sections is the enclosed humidity filled greenhouses. The stalks of vegetables growing green under the bright bulbs remind me of my grandfather's tales of the earth he dreamed about before the loss of the sun.

I take pleasure in the simple things, like running my hand over the rough texture of wood products that survived the freezing of the planet. Several buildings still make use of doors fashioned from the long extinct trees that once covered large sections of earth.

One cold dark day found Annaliese and I standing on the surface observing the preparations as a team of men from Adams Mountain load supplies and equipment into a motorized ice sled. The team ready to lead an expedition to a colony far across the frozen sea of ice.

I stand lost in thought as I stare into the shifting winds, remembering back to the days when I, too, had travelled over these vast expanses of snow and ice under the skies obscured by volcanic dust when Annaliese lets out a startled cry.

Taken by surprise, I glance over at her face. A bright light reflects off her visor. Annaliese's head is tilted back and her face turned up to the sky watching something over my shoulder. Her arm is outstretched and pointing skyward. I spin around to see the source of her excitement.

For almost two centuries, the skies over the earth have remained dark, choked by dust and storm clouds. I stand tight to Annaliese holding her hand, the two of us, with eyes turned skyward, we marvel at a sight I never thought possible in my lifetime. A sight I've often dreamed, but never imagined. The clouds and dust above have parted, exposing a patch of blue sky and a single column of sunlight smiles down on us.

The time passes. Annaliese is often busy with her duties away from the palace. She now carries our child. The doctors tell us it's a boy. Annaliese insists that we name our child after my father.

On this particular evening, I venture down to the depths of the palace. A room I had no previous desire to return to, but tonight I was on another adventure. The day the prophets' rule ended all those months ago, and I found Annaliese and her father in this room, I had noticed a shelf set against the back wall. In my wounded state, I gazed at that shelf while I waited for help to come. I had forgotten about it and not ventured down into the basement since, but now as things have taken on a more mundane routine, my curiosity drifts back down those stairs to what captured my curiosity on that shelf.

I tread carefully down the long staircase. Lights are ablaze, brightening my path. Hesitating at the bottom, I step into the room and wander over to the shelf.

Books. Actual paper bound books. I lean close and blow dust off some of the bindings. The titles are unfamiliar. Then one catches my interest. I slip it from its shelf and read the cover. The book is a history of the last war ever fought on earth, THE CLIMATE WARS.

Richard Cozicar

Richard Cozicar

Going Silent

Retired CSIS operative turned fishing guide Brand Coldstream is forced back into action when he narrowly survives an attempt on his life. Not knowing who to trust, Brand is forced underground as he investigates his would-be assassins and their connection to his old unit and their last big operation, which ended under very suspicious circumstances.

From North Vancouver to the shipping ports of Montreal, Going Silent is an exciting, modern thriller that follows Coldstream as he works to uncover a conspiracy that goes back longer, and up higher, than he ever imagined.

For more info, visit richardcozicar.com

Buy Online today

SILENT CRUSADE
A BRAND COLDSTREAM NOVEL
RICHARD COZICAR

Silent Crusade

The end of a weeklong fishing trip and Brand Coldstream is rested and ready to head back to the business of the bustling city and the arms of his girlfriend, Sara Monahan.

As he leaves the peace and seclusion of the outdoors, his world slowly unravels. Repeated attempts to contact Sara on his flight back to civilization go unheeded. Disappointment is replaced by concern when the retired CSIS agent discovers Sara's house empty, her whereabouts unknown.

Instincts bred from years of working for Canada's premier intelligence agency send Brand on a desperate search for his missing girlfriend. Brand quickly discovers that her disappearance may be the tip of the iceberg in a centuries-old feud between two rival factions.

What connection does the kidnapping of a computer researcher and a secret Cabal have in common? And what part could Sara possibly play in the developing plot? The trail of the abduction leads Brand on a cross border mystery that puts him in the middle of a religious war,
a battle waged in the deep shadows
and corporate boardrooms.

In a plot so devious, can the world survive the consequences as the religious battle draws to a close? Only one man has what it takes to straddle the fine line of the law in order to stop the sworn enemies from destroying each other and world peace.

Richard Cozicar

About the Author

A Canadian author in the Mystery Thriller genre. Skilled carpenter and avid fly fisher. Collector of music, movies, books, and all things Elvis.

Contact Information:

Twitter: @RichardCozicar

www.facebook.com/RichardCozicar

richardcozicar@gmail.com

www.richardcozicar.com

www.ingramcontent.com/pod-product-compliance
Lightning Source LLC
Chambersburg PA
CBHW052353060726
47592CB00020B/2140